T0162529

Nellcott Is My Darling

Nellcott Is My Darling

GOLDA FRIED

Coach House Books

First edition, fourth printing, January 2006

Published with the assistance of the Canada Council for the Arts and the Ontario Arts Council. We also acknowledge the Government of Ontario through the Ontario Book Publishing Tax Credit Program and the Government of Canada through the Book Publishing Industry Development Program.

LIBRARY AND ARCHIVES CANADA
CATALOGUING IN PUBLICATION

Fried, Golda, 1972-
Nellcott is my darling / Golda Fried.

ISBN 1-55245-151-8

I. Title.

PS8561.R4915N45 2005   C813'.54   C2005-901690-6

'I don't think I'm ever going to figure it out.'
– Elliott Smith

*A*lice sat in one of the hard plastic chairs in the lecture hall at McGill University; only when the lights went out did she feel comfortable. The movie started. No commercials. No previews. Just a faraway sound.

She was wearing black and a worn leather jacket that she thought was a moss green but other people had told her it was brown.

The movie came on. It was *The Graduate*.

She was just starting her Bachelor of Arts degree.

She loved the sixties though it was the early nineties now. Katharine Ross in the movie had straight long dark hair. Alice had long hair that was mostly curly and got frizzy in the rain. She liked Julie Christie hair and Ali MacGraw hair.

In the darkness, she could laugh out loud and sound like a duck.

In the movie, there was a shot where the camera zoomed from Dustin Hoffman's face to a monkey and Alice laughed again. Watching people was like watching monkeys at the zoo. Dustin Hoffman was driving around like a maniac with sideburns. She loved it.

She wondered if the day would come when a guy would drive up to her door panicked and she would smile because she knew their love was solid.

The Film Society showed movies for a dollar four nights a week from Wednesday to Saturday and Alice had been to every one that first week.

Movies made her forget that she was a virgin still. That she was only pretending to be an adult. That she still had so far to go.

Her room at the dorm was a closet at the end of the hall and was extremely white. It smelled like fresh paint. She was not good at decorating. Other girls on her floor brought lampshades that matched their bedspreads and their wastepaper baskets.

She ripped a photo of David Lynch, the movie director, out of a *People* magazine and taped it to the wall. In the photo, David Lynch was standing on the ground diagonally. It was impossible to stand like that. She looked at the photo lying on her bed with her head cocked to the side. Maybe it was possible.

It was a utilitarian room: a single bed, with a mattress that looked lumpy and had blue stripes going down it. A desk by the window with a view of a tree. A wooden dresser with a funky smell. The tiniest fridge by the closet, a fridge for a few cans of pop at best.

She took out a memo pad from her knapsack and wrote: *sheets*.

She plugged in her ghetto blaster but, for the first time, she didn't immediately put rock music on. She listened for new sounds.

Alice had come all the way from Toronto to go to school in Montreal. She couldn't believe her parents had let her go.

Her mom had cried as Alice was packing her duffel bag like she was going off to war. 'My baby, my baby, my baby,' her mom said.

Her mom was a romantic. She always waved at the door to loved ones until they were completely out of sight.

She said to Alice, 'I bet you get a boyfriend right away. I bet you can't live without one.'

Alice looked at her mom strangely. It was a weird thing to say. Alice had never had a boyfriend. She was quiet and had worn her dad's baggy sweaters to high school.

'I don't think so, Mom,' is what she said.

When her mom was mad, her dad would disappear until her mood changed. Her dad would raise his eyebrows so his eyes would pop out, his cheer-up face. His far-sighted glasses magnified his eyes so they looked even bigger. He was like one of Alice's stuffed animals with googly eyes. Her mom would eventually smile and Alice would breathe normally again.

Her dad had walked into the bedroom carrying what looked like a dead animal. 'Here, you can have my parka for those wintry days.' He put the coat in her arms. It weighed a ton. He was always trying to give her his things.

Alice said, 'This parka takes up a whole duffel bag by itself.'

'James McGill, James McGill. We are all the sons of James McGill,' he cheered and did a little dance. He had gone to McGill. Maybe that was why she was allowed to go.

'I'm a daughter,' Alice said, exasperated.

Her dad looked at her a minute and said, 'You are? Okay,' and smiled on. 'Let's see what else I can give you. You want to take this pen?' He held out a pen in front of her nose that was advertising someone's insurance business. She took the pen.

'Take this too,' her mom said. It was a baby-blue plastic laundry basket. Alice placed her ghetto blaster in it. 'It's a laundry basket.' Her mom looked worried.

Alice was a quiet sort. She had eccentric grandmothers to live up to and had never done her own laundry.

Now here she was, going to some nook and cranny in a Student Centre in Montreal; Alice felt like a little teacup full of fear.

The Film Society was on the third level of the Student Centre, past the yearbook committee, past the drama club, past the washrooms. The Film Society was on its way out.

She stood in the doorway gazing in. Kids had always said she had a staring problem.

The room was white with no movie posters. It had one metal cabinet with books on film theory from the sixties. There was a stack of phone books on the floor and a couple of bright orange seventies-looking chairs.

There was also a guy with a bike helmet on who was banging around in the cabinet. He said his name was William. He had been in the Film Society last year.

She wanted to go in and put her knapsack down; it was full of her new textbooks and weighed a ton. It was navy and had the big red and white McGill crest on it. Her dad had bought it for her when they checked the campus out together the year before.

'Film Society elections are on Friday. Come back,' William said, sizing her up.

'What are the positions?' she stammered.

'President, publicity, events coordinator, accountant and secretary. But forget about president. I'm going to be that.'

Secretary, she thought. *I could probably do that.* She stood in the doorway hooking her thumbs under the straps of the knapsack like she couldn't leave.

'Okay, come back Friday,' he said.

When Alice was little, her dad used to rent a film projector from the North York Fairview Library for her birthday parties. The films would be scary: pirates with rotting teeth who chased after children. One movie was an animated version of a child going to Hell. Her dad would unfold the screen up on the stand like a magic trick. He would let her clip the film before the projector ate it. Then she would watch the film go through the projector from the side of the machine. She would see her dad in front of the projector light, big as a mountain, waving his arm and saying, 'All the kids on the sleeping bags.'

Alice was in love with the orange chairs in the Film Society room. They made her feel like she was at a birthday party in a kid's playroom with plastic furniture or at least in the seventies, which had better fashion. She couldn't wait to be back there.

Between classes and meals at the dorm cafeteria, she waited in bookstores. She hung out in the library. The library was her church. She prayed in the stacks that she could pass her freshman year. She felt the covers of some of the old cloth books.

Finally it was five on Friday and she was on one of those orange chairs in the Film Society office.

William was wearing a name tag for the occasion. There were five positions and only five people there, but William went through the motions.

'Alice Charles for secretary. All those in favour say *aye*.'

A flare shot up inside her. Her fingers grabbed on to the seat of her orange chair. People said *aye*. She heard them.

Rally became the events coordinator. Rally was a girl with raven-black hair who never smiled and was reading Tom Robbins' *Jitterbug Perfume* before the meeting. She was eating some carrot-macaroni salad from a mayonnaise jar.

'Did you make that yourself?' Alice said.

'Yeah,' Rally said, like it was no big deal.

Robert became the accountant. He had slick short hair, khaki pants and a button-down shirt. He looked like Henry Fonda. He spoke quietly but in a way that showed he was dead sure he was right. Alice hated that kind of confidence. Everyone should know they couldn't always be right.

Casey, publicity, was wearing rollerblades and no helmet. He couldn't sit still. He probably rollerbladed in his sleep.

William reached out and shook hands with everyone. The boys got patted on the back as well.

William said, 'Okay, each of us will have to take turns selling tickets. Alice, you make some sort of schedule to make this happen.'

Alice watched Rally fishing out pens from the bottom of her weightless-looking over-the-shoulder messenger bag. Alice's knapsack had so much in it that it was crushing her toe.

William said, 'No, scratch that. I'll just take the schedule, post it on this wall, and everyone has to put their name on it at least two nights a week.'

Robert said, 'I have a list here of what movies we should run.'

Rally said, 'I'm the events coordinator; I'm picking the movies.'

'We're all picking the movies,' William said.

Alice ripped a piece of paper from her Abnormal Psychology notebook and, as the movies were mentioned, she wrote everything down. She looked at her handwriting and how she wrote on the page. She was developing a handwriting style.

When she looked up, she caught Robert turning his eyes away from hers fast. Alice hated that. It made her feel like he didn't want her to exist. Like she might like him or something.

William said, '*Citizen Kane* is an important movie, but will anyone come out for that?'

'Who cares what the students want? We must go forth and educate,' Rally said.

'We have to survive,' William said, impatient with all of them already. 'It's 1991. People are starting to own VCRs and stay home.'

'It's not the same as seeing it on the big screen,' Alice said. They all looked at her. It was the first time she had spoken.

When she got back to her dorm, she called her parents with wild abandon. 'I'm secretary of the Film Society!'

'Hold on a second,' her dad said. 'Your mom got a dog to replace you and it's going to bite me.'

'He's not going to bite you.' She could hear her mom in the background.

'It's nipping at my leg,' her dad said, dropping the phone.

Alice stared at her baby-blue plastic laundry basket on the floor. It was piling up already.

The Film Society was showing *Bonnie and Clyde*. Alice had never seen it before. Her mother had given her a blank journal to write down all her expenses so she could budget herself. So far, all she had been able to do was write a list of movies she had to see before she died. *Bonnie and Clyde* was in there. Probably because her favourite high school English teacher, Mr. Krackle, had mentioned it.

'It's most unimpressive,' Bethany said. Bethany was Alice's high school friend. She was talking about the fact that they'd be watching the film in the uncomfortable chairs of the lecture hall.

Bethany stood around fidgeting while Alice sold tickets right outside the lecture hall. Red tickets went out of Alice's hand like she was giving people candy. The students came in groups, dropping large bills like it was nothing to them. William scrambled to get change from customers in line. Most people wore blue jeans and had their hands comfortably in their front pockets. When they got inside the lecture hall, they hurdled over the backs of the lecture chairs and fell into them.

'What's this film about?' Bethany asked Alice. 'Is this a horror film? I can't handle a horror film.'

'It's not *Friday the 13th*,' Alice said. 'I heard it's about bank robbers. But it's okay because they're in love.'

The movie started. All the movies the Film Society got were old and crackly. The sound came across as if travelling down a long corridor. Alice leaned in the doorway. 'Go sit down,' she said to Bethany.

'You're not going to sit with me?'

'I have to wait for stragglers,' Alice said. Bethany took a seat. 'It's a decent turnout,' Alice said to William.

William was counting heads. There were maybe twenty people there. He said, 'We had to pay the projectionist. We had to rent the copy of the film. We're way in the red, Alice. Give me the cash box.' William left with the cash box. It was a little kid's piggy bank. And there were stragglers. The stragglers got in for free.

Alice walked down the thin lecture-hall steps, trying to find her balance in the dark, and joined Bethany.

'You guys should really sell popcorn at these movies,' Bethany said.

'Uh-huh,' Alice answered, but she was already absorbed by the movie.

In the movie, Bonnie wore a negligee in her first scene. She spoke to Clyde in this negligee and thought nothing of getting in the car with him and driving off. It quickly became a movie of a girl running away from home.

'No girl would really get in a car with a stranger,' Bethany whispered.

Alice thought that it would be so hard for her to make a final break from her own parents. A guy would have to come up to her bedroom and carry her out. The guy would have to be pretty fearless.

A few times Bethany said 'That's disgusting' or 'Alice' as if Alice were hurting her. Sally Struthers was showing cleavage and eating a chicken leg in one scene. In another, somebody lost an eye. Bethany was putting her hands over her eyes and making freak-out sounds. It was making Alice a nervous wreck. She felt responsible for whether or not Bethany liked the film.

There was one scene where everyone looked like they were in heaven, right before they died.

'The director filmed this scene with a silk stocking over the camera,' Alice heard a guy two rows down say. She made a mental note to go to the fifth floor of the McLennan Library and look for books on the director, Arthur Penn, sometime soon.

Then there was a shot of tumbleweed rolling and a shot of birds flying out of a tree.

After the movie, Alice was spinning. 'What an ending, can you believe it? The birds were their souls! The birds were their souls flying out of the tree like a soul flying out of the body.' She wanted to crash right into Bethany.

Bethany was stewing. 'Honestly, I think movies should make you laugh. Movies should just entertain – that's it,' she said. 'Honestly, that movie was just about violence.'

'I've never met a guy named Clyde. Have you?' Alice asked her.

'Who cares? Now I wouldn't want to.'

'Bethany, that was a great movie.'

'I feel gross. I want to go home and take a shower.'

There were no birds in the night air on Alice's way home. They were all in her head.

Alice undressed for bed thinking of Bonnie's negligee. She had only one piece of lingerie, a cream-coloured slip her mother had bought for her to wear under a party dress when she was thirteen.

Some people could wear those things to bed, she guessed. She always wore a T-shirt and men's pyjama bottoms.

She walked out of her room and into the hallway barefoot. She liked to walk around barefoot. Socks always felt like they were saran-wrapped to her feet. The dorm had a sickly grey carpet and was well-heated; otherwise she probably could not have pulled this off.

Allegra's door was open; she was in the room beside Alice's and Alice went in. Allegra was an artist. She saved gum wrappers for future art projects. On the wall, she had collages made of prints of old art reproductions, stolen menus and shiny parts from the gold and red foil off rich chocolates. It was her version of quilting, Alice guessed. She lay her head down on one of Allegra's purple throw pillows on the floor.

Allegra kept reading her book of poetry with the German original lines on the left and the English translations on the right as Alice stared around the room.

The first time Alice had seen Allegra she was wearing a body-fitting red Chinese silk dress with combat boots and her hair uplifted so her bottle-blond strands poked out perfectly. Alice just stared at her in the hallway, holding on to her own elbows. The guy who had come to pick Allegra up looked at her and nodded but acted like her outfit was nothing extraordinary. And they were just going to movies.

Now Allegra had on her signature black silk men's pyjama top and men's wool pinstriped pants with combat boots. She was so happy that she had found coffee beans called Boom. She kept telling Alice her coffee was called Boom. Alice liked how Allegra swallowed up her favourite words like bonbons. *Boom* was just one of them; she also liked *decadent*, *divine* and *luscious* and she referred to talking on the telephone as being on *the blower*.

From the way Allegra's room was positioned, Alice got a full-size view of the big light-bulbed cross that stood on Mount Royal and was lit up in the night.

'How can you sleep with that cross in the window?' Alice asked her.

'I love it.' She smiled a big lipstick smile. 'It makes me think I'm living in a cathedral.'

Allegra had red votive candles along her window ledge. There was a diaphanous lilac scarf draped over the window. There was seductive lighting from vintage lamps. There was so much to look at.

Maybe Alice was staring too long. Allegra's room was really a wonderland, complete with fairy dust in pill bottles and feathers and notes in jars.

'I need some more Boom,' Allegra said and got up from the bed.

Alice would see Allegra walking down the hall with a coffee pot all the time. Allegra would float down the hallway with it and then return to her room and shut the door. Allegra drank coffee all day and shook all night like a butterfly caught between two panes of glass in a window. When she flipped pages in her address book, her hands would slightly tremble.

When she was gone, Alice rolled over and looked into Allegra's shoebox of tapes which she kept under the bed. She had every Tom Waits album. Some Nick Cave. The Pixies' *Supernova*.

Allegra came back with the coffee pot and Cricket rushed in after her. Alice quickly took her hand out of the shoebox.

'And then I laughed in the salesperson's face and demanded he give me another plant for free,' Cricket said. Her voice was extremely loud. Cricket wore skirts that rustled when she sped down the hall or rugby outfits with Christmas colours and stripes. Alice didn't think she was artsy enough to be in the same room with Allegra. 'Come, help me place these plants in my room so they get the most light,' Cricket said to Allegra.

When they came back, Alice still hadn't moved.

'Can you fucking believe the editors of *Cosmo* want us to tape our breasts for cleavage?' Cricket was still shouting in Allegra's ear.

'I think the standing in the shower under ice-cold water for fifteen minutes to make your breasts as perky as possible was worse,' Allegra said.

'Allegra, you are my best friend,' Cricket said. 'Next semester, we've got to leave all these losers in this dorm and get our own place.'

Alice wondered if Allegra and Cricket liked her at all.

Cricket woke up three times a week at five in the morning to play rugby. Alice had seen her jog back at seven with an orange segment in her mouth like a mouthguard.

Cricket screamed when she got her period, and then Allegra started doing it too. They hugged each other dramatically.

Allegra would take walks on the mountain alone, even though legend had it that a naked guy in a raincoat flashed people there.

Who were these girls and where did they come from?

Allegra ended up being from Nova Scotia where she hadn't learned French at all. However, soon she was dating a French guy who didn't speak more than ten words of English. Once Alice saw Allegra making out with the French guy in the hall. Alice must have slowed to a full stop.

'Don't look at me like that,' Allegra said to Alice as the guy kissed her neck.

One day Allegra had gotten the French guy's watch. She just slipped it off his wrist and put it on hers and then she owned it. It was a man's watch, metal and clunky and big, and Alice thought Allegra looked powerful wearing it. Women's watches were dainty with a thin strap and numbers too small to read.

'That's it,' Alice said. When she wanted something it took over her mind. She went down to St. Catherine Street where all the main stores lined up in a row. She bought herself a man's watch very similar to the one Allegra had. She could hear her mother's voice in her ear saying that she had no identity of her own, that she was just copying everyone else. *At least I'm copying an artist*, she told herself.

She started showering at night to avoid everyone in the morning.

The best thing about being away from home was using her mail key on the square metal mailbox next to everyone else's and getting letters.

Her dad typed his with his two index fingers because his handwriting was so illegible. He wrote things like 'Dinner tonight was salad with lettuce.'

Her mom wrote ones that were flowery and many pages long. She also wrote what she made for dinner.

A lot of times in the mailbox there would be another pizza place advertising its menu. Alice hadn't ordered one yet but she'd seen a few people do it and the pizzas always came with this dough ball in the middle that seemed to be holding the pizza box up. She'd never seen that in Toronto.

The worst thing about the dorm was the noise level, which unnerved her, especially from this one guy who seemed to turn into a cowboy when he was drunk. When there was a McGill football game, the shrieking got unbearable. Cricket came back from one game with her face painted half white and half red. She could have been an extra in *Apocalypse Now*.

And every week there seemed to be a new health problem going around, like pink eye or this sickness that gave you white spots on the back of your throat. This week it was the worst: crabs. Allegra swore she got it from a toilet seat.

Alice always thought she was coming down with something but she never missed a class.

Alice had signed up for Children's Literature though she had never had an affinity for children. It was supposed to be a bird class, a no-brainer.

The class was in the same lecture room where the Film Society showed movies, the Leacock Auditorium, but the room was a little more intimidating during the day.

The lecturer had pages and pages of notes. He looked like a Santa Claus who didn't give a shit.

On different levels going up like a coliseum, there were about two hundred students around him in chairs with right-hand armrests. The students were a flock of birds in front of him flapping pages.

There was one guy who had caught Alice's eye. He had long piano hands that he'd slowly rub together when someone else was talking. He sat in the last row near where she walked in. He slouched in his chair but always had his chin tilted up like the overhead lights were giving him a tan. He always sat next to mean-looking friends who snickered.

She sat near him but never next to him. She felt contagious around him. She just wasn't cool enough.

She told Bethany about him. He had a name but now his name was the Children's Lit guy.

'The Children's Lit guy snubbed me again today,' she told Bethany. 'I'm going to the movies to feel better.'

Alice went to the movies at regular theatres on top of Film Society showings, sometimes even alone. Nothing could have prepared her for *Wild at Heart*. Not even that *People* magazine profile of its director, David Lynch. She was so thankful Bethany hadn't been with her; there was one scene where a guy's head was bashed on the floor. If she had taken Bethany, their friendship would be over. While Alice sat through the movie, the contact-lens solution in her bag leaked on her arm and she didn't even notice until the credits were on.

At night in her dorm room, she didn't think anyone would listen to her as a film director. She cried on the phone to her father that she would really prefer to be at a film school somewhere like maybe New York or even Toronto where her high school friend Walker went to Ryerson for film, but her father said no; it would lead nowhere and she needed a university degree. Her mom agreed. After the conversation ended she did somersaults on the bed to shake up the sadness that was in her head.

She called Walker. Walker was cavalier. In her mind, Alice was always begging him, 'Send me mixed tapes, tell me what movies to watch, tell me what you learn in film school.' She wanted to know.

When Alice's dad had dropped her off at high school in the mornings, she would go straight to the cafeteria. Walker was also dropped off early. He would sit up on a cafeteria table before the first bell rang and push back his black fifties glasses up the bridge of his nose. He used his hands a lot while describing his film shots at the dramatic moments of the story, and almost every moment was dramatic. His hair which was long and brown would flip back like a hi-hat on a drum set.

She would watch those hands and that hair and smile.

He would make films using Super 8 cameras that did not record sound. He relied on facial expressions to tell his story.

He let Alice float around him but he kept his distance. She had never been over to his house, for instance.

One time, just to know him a little better, Alice interviewed him for a class assignment. She used a hand-held cassette recorder and everything. He talked through the whole ninety-minute tape. He talked Kubrick, Penn, Scorsese and Coppola. He talked Jim Morrison. He talked Jack Kerouac and Henry Miller. The play button popped out and the tape stopped rolling and then the interview was over. And Alice was sad it was over because she didn't think she could ask him any more personal questions after that without the pretense of an interview.

Somehow their relationship carried over into their freshman year. She couldn't say why. Relationships were the greatest mysteries of all time. She would never figure them out.

When she called Walker from her dorm room long distance, he always made her wait while he made a cup of coffee or lit a cigarette.

This time he asked her, 'So, have you lost your virginity yet?'

She laughed nervously. 'What?'

'Well?' This was someone who had already pulled a lot of girls.

'No,' she said.

'I'm dating a model.' He had never offered to have sex with Alice. She was very aware of that. She waited for more about the model. 'Only this model has a boyfriend, but she keeps jumping me in the elevator at school. I think she might even be married.'

'There's a Children's Lit guy I like.'

'What's a Children's Lit guy?'

'Someone in my Children's Literature class.'

'Do you picture having sex with him?'

'No, it stops at kissing. It's like I want to reach out and touch a wave but I don't want it to wash over me.'

'Do you have any sexy underwear?'

'I doubt it.'

'Maybe that should be your first step.'

After that conversation, Alice opened the top drawer of her wooden dresser and checked out her underwear. She had about ten cotton pairs that her mom had bought her in bulk. She got out a pair of scissors and cut the little bows off all of them.

Alice followed Rally to a party after a Film Society meeting. Rally called the corner convenience store *the dep*, short for *dépanneur*, and made them buy some cheap merlot. Rally was wearing black everything, including black combat boots. Alice was wearing black lace underwear she had gotten for the occasion and they were scratchy as hell.

The party was way up Parc Avenue in a section of town called the Plateau. When they reached the place there was this whimsical wrought-iron gate that came up to their knees, a child's gate, with a latch to open before they went up a little walkway to the front door. Loud chatter and the boom of a bass line came from behind the door. Alice looked up at the full moon and gave a hopeful smile.

When they walked in, everything about the place impressed her. There were hardwood floors and high ceilings with thick mouldings around the edges that looked like frosting around a cake. There were posters of Toulouse-Lautrec dancing girls on the wall. There were white lace curtains covering the windows. There was a chandelier above her head in the main hallway and Alice almost fell over looking at it.

She didn't know anyone else at the party. She followed Rally to the kitchen and just watched as people came and put cartons of Boréal and St. Ambroise in the fridge. The cupboards in the kitchen had glass panels so you could see all the cans of beans and dry goods that the girls who lived there had.

One guy grabbed her elbow and started talking to her. It puzzled her.

He had brown eyes like Alice only he had black eyeliner under them. She felt self-conscious that she was wearing no makeup; she wished there was such a thing as Halloween for adults, where you could go trick-or-treating and someone would dump makeup into your bag, so she would own a respectable amount instead of just the free samples her mom had passed on.

'You know, you walked by me earlier,' he told her, 'and all I saw was your feet and your sandals. And I just followed the sandals.'

Yes, she was wearing sandals and it was a cold fall already and she had no business wearing sandals, but they were comfortable.

He was wearing a white shirt with the cuffs open, the kind that would dangle molecules away from the butter if he reached for a roll at the breakfast table. He also had black pointy boots.

'It's so weird. I never like hippie girls with sandals,' he said.

'What's wrong with sandals? Who are you?'

'Nellcott Ragland.'

'I'm Alice Charles,' she said.

He led her through the yellow kitchen to a living room that was painted apple-green and pulled her down to the hardwood floor. They both sat facing each other, hugging their knees. She was used to white rooms and carpet.

He was so energetic, shaking his cigarettes until they finally exploded out of the pack. He put one in her mouth.

She didn't smoke. She twirled it in her fingers like a mini-baton. She thought he had sunflower eyes because they were dark brown and because his eyelashes were long and thick and curled outward.

He spent five minutes stuffing the cigarettes back in the pack like he was nervous.

She found out that he was not in school – he worked at a record store and played guitar – so they talked about music. Alice had definite opinions about rock music. She had listened to her fair share of QI07 ROCK growing up in Toronto, and especially to the station's *Psychedelic Sundays*.

Of course, he had his own definite opinions about music too, and their first conversation was an argument.

'"Simple Twist of Fate" is the best song on *Blood on the Tracks*,' she said. She knew her Bob Dylan.

'No way. It's definitely "Tangled up in Blue,"' he said.

His shirt was buttoned but only at the bottom, so his chest hair showed a bit. She normally preferred guys with no chest hair and was embarrassed seeing it. His pants were tight, like black stirrup pants for horseback riding. His arm was muscular as he brought a beer bottle to his lips and pulled on it.

At one point she got up and looked at the food table. There were pita wedges with hummus dip and a chip bowl.

There were girls in vintage dresses who looked like walking wallpaper.

There was that Mount Royal cross in the window looking over her.

'Are you okay?' Rally said. 'You look a little pale.'

'I shouldn't have worn sandals,' Alice said. 'My feet are numb.'

'Just drink a little more wine,' Rally said.

Alice really wanted some food but was scared of having hummus as it was a communal dipping bowl. She wanted to get over this fear. She didn't want to be pristine. She grabbed a wedge of pita, dipped it in and brought it up to her mouth. She imagined cold sores blossoming on her lips.

Whoever lived in this apartment loved to read. They made extra shelves for books with planks of wood sandwiched with loose bricks. Alice scanned the titles.

Nellcott came and found her and grabbed her arm. He wouldn't let her leave with Rally until he got her phone number and until she agreed to go on a date with him the next night. She told him her room was the third-storey corner window at the top of the hill in the highest dorm.

He knew her name was Alice but he just called her *darling*.

Rally smiled knowingly on their way out the door.

'So, you and Nellcott?' Rally said.

'Yeah,' Alice said. They were near the bagel factory on St. Urbain Street. Alice could smell the fresh dough in the air.

Rally said, 'I hope you like sex, drugs and rock and roll.'

Alice stopped in the middle of the street, panicked like she had lost her keys. 'What do I do when he wants to have sex with me?'

'You're not asking me how to have sex, are you?' Rally said.

'No.'

'Well, good. I'm not good at drawing pictures.'

'No chance he's a virgin too?'

'You're really a virgin in this day and age?'

'Can we focus on what I'm going to do?'

'He's had loads of sex, for sure. Maybe he wants something else. If you don't want to give him sex, maybe that's okay.'

'Is he a nice guy?'

'Yeah, I heard he's really nice. The kind who bakes cookies for his grandmother,' Rally said.

Alice was quiet walking in the gutter. 'What's going to happen to me, Rally? Is this guy going to make me pregnant and drop out of university?'

'Don't give a guy that much power,' was all she said.

For Alice, getting ready for a date meant slapping on some blue jeans, wearing a tight black top and maybe some mascara. She didn't think she'd ever seen Allegra wear jeans.

In Alice's preparation, there was no perfume, no silk stockings, no collection of beaded necklaces. No dumping of the closet onto the bed.

No purses. Purses were for people who wanted to get mugged.

She waited by her windowsill for Nellcott. When Alice smelled love in the air, it wasn't the type of love that would comfort her or hold her or ask her if she was okay. It was a crazy love like an accordion player who would show up under her window outside and play for her in the rain.

He was taking forever. She went over to her closet to see if there was something better she could wear.

Rocks hit the window. She looked down. Nellcott was swinging from a tree branch. Then he was trying to climb up but the limbs were too fragile.

She went down to meet him, passing people on the stairs to whom she said, in her head, *I've got a date. I've got a date; isn't that weird?* Like they cared.

Nellcott and Alice went down the hill and then up Parc Avenue and then into a diner. He hadn't talked much. He had walked a couple steps ahead of her looking straight ahead and hadn't grabbed for her hand. But in the booth he sat back and stared right at her.

She guessed diners could be romantic but the lighting in this one was all wrong. Instead of candlelight, blaring in-your-face fluorescent lights illuminated all the ancient stains on the plastic tabletops.

The waitress was a lady in her sixties with red red lipstick and an angry pen. 'What do you want to drink?' she asked them.

'Coffee,' Alice said. She wasn't brought up with coffee but it was all around her as a student. She knew that she liked coffee with cream and sugar.

'I'll have water,' he said.

'Don't you drink coffee?' she asked.

'No, I don't drink the stuff.' She was the lethargic one and he was manic. It didn't make any sense.

Nellcott ordered a Montreal smoked-meat sandwich on rye with potato pancakes.

'Do you want applesauce or sour cream with that?' the waitress asked him.

'Both,' Alice answered. She didn't order any food. She wanted to eat his.

Alice reached for the ketchup but then she remembered they hadn't ordered fries and put it back on the side.

As they waited for their drinks to come, Nellcott reached over to the metal bowl of creamers and took one. He ripped back the paper top and swallowed the half-and-half in one gulp like a whiskey shot. He did this two more times as Alice stared at him in wonder.

The menu was a paper menu that served as a placemat as well. Nellcott turned it over and took out a pen from inside his beat-up leather jacket. He started clicking the pen on and off while staring at her. Finally, he wrote a question for her on the placemat in the margins. She took the pen and wrote back. It was kind of fun.

Even Nellcott's handwriting looked like he had just crawled out of bed.

He told her he either wanted to live on a farm or buy a van and drive all over the country, living out of it.

'Well, which one are you leaning towards?'

'I'm still deciding,' he said.

Then he doodled and she made him sign it like it was a very important piece of art.

He wrote on her paper placemat, 'There is one of us now, you know.'

He wanted her soul from the beginning.

They walked out of the diner aimlessly checking each other out. He ripped a marigold out of someone's flowerbox and gave it to her. She smelled it, made a wish and threw it over the person's fence. He ripped another one and put it behind his ear like a cigarette.

Now he grabbed her hand but only to drag her into oncoming traffic. She hesitated, even dug her heels in the ground, but he kept pulling her, saying jaywalking was part of living in Montreal, saying the cars would have to stop.

He wanted to go out drinking at the Bifteck but it was getting late and she had school the next day. He started to get all shifty with his eyes when they were back at the dorm and rocked on his boot heels with his hands down the back pockets of his jeans.

She was uncomfortable too. She was wearing her black lace underwear for the second day in a row.

'Okay, then,' she said and ran inside the glass doors.

A lice sat on her bed and wasn't tired for once. Her sandals came off and then her jeans, and then she flung her lace underwear in the air.

She even thought about calling her mother but killed that idea pretty fast.

Did she even know his last name? (Ragland.) What did he do? (He worked at a record store.) What did he like to eat? (Meat and potatoes. Finicky eater. She had made him talk about this in detail. He would eat every kind of red meat but the veins in chicken wings made him squeamish. And mushrooms made him want to vomit. His favourite meal was something called *hamburger steak* with brown, thick gravy all over it. Alice didn't understand; how could something be a hamburger and a steak?)

There was this couple in high school that was Alice's idea of true love. They were a year older than Alice. They both had brown ringlets in their hair that came down to their shoulders. They both had pure white skin like they never ate pizza or cheeseburgers. Alice would guess that the saying was true: if two people spend all their time together, they start looking like each other.

The boy never talked about his girlfriend to anyone, like that was sacred information. It was a very good sign to Alice that love existed.

What Alice remembered was watching that couple dance at the prom. There was nothing awkward about their dancing.

They really seemed free. The song, of course, was ridiculous: Meatloaf's 'Paradise by the Dashboard Light.'

At one point, the guy was trying to tell the girl something. He pulled her close to him by her wrist and cupped his other hand over her ear. She shook her head. She couldn't hear him. He thought it was maybe all her thick brown hair so he delicately took strands of her hair and placed them behind her ear. She still couldn't hear him so she dragged him down to the floor as if it were quieter down there, and they huddled together in the middle of the dance floor with everyone dancing around them.

Alice heard they went to university and broke up.

This Nellcott feeling she woke up with was making Alice feel sick. She rushed to the science library to go find Bethany. Bethany was a political-science student but studied in the science library because it was quieter. She was that serious. The place was darker than the McLennan Library, and as Alice rushed past the rows and rows of students quietly studying in carrels, she was struck with the urge to become a mad whistler, but she kept it to herself.

She finally found Bethany at one of the big tables with three other people. Bethany had a textbook open with three different highlighters going. Her hair was all pulled back from her face in a ponytail and she had the end of a pen in her mouth. Bethany was unapproachable but she was Alice's friend.

'Bethany, you've got to come record-shopping with me now.' Bethany was slow to move. 'I met this guy. He works at Basement Records. I'll buy you a Coke.' Bethany drank at least five Cokes a day, starting at breakfast.

'Look after my stuff,' Bethany said to a girl at her table. 'I'm not going to be long.'

Basement Records was right next to a Dunkin' Donuts downtown but it was sub-street level: they had to go down some stairs to get there. The whole store was underground and as they walked in, Alice was sure Bethany was thinking that she was going into the depths of hell or that the ceiling in the store was too low or that the whole building was going to collapse on her.

Bethany was claustrophobic. Alice didn't see Nellcott at first and started looking at records.

'Do you even have a record player?' Nellcott had sneaked up behind her.

Alice hadn't seen him but now all of a sudden her hand, which was holding up a Leonard Cohen album, started to shake. She was going to put it back but he snatched it. She looked over at Bethany. She was looking at a CD but her lips were in a straight line.

'I'm just looking,' she said, taking the record out of his hands and putting it back.

Alice looked back at Nellcott. He towered over her and sort of rocked on his Cuban heels. He had a chunky silver bracelet on his right wrist.

'What have you been doing?' he asked her.

'Since last night?'

He leaned over and kissed her on the cheek. She smiled.

'How 'bout as a wedding present, I let you pick out a hundred records.'

'Who will I be getting married to?'

He didn't answer. He went over to ring up a customer. Alice noticed that he kept an ashtray on top of the cash register so he could smoke whenever he wanted to. A cigarette was burning in it right now. Bethany coughed from across the store.

'Alice, I've got to go back now,' Bethany shouted.

'I've got to go,' Alice said to Nellcott as he was walking back to her.

She tried to walk out casually. She felt like she had a big bow on her butt when she turned around and walked up the stairs knowing he was watching.

On the street, Bethany said, 'He looks like he just walked off a plank.'

'I like him,' Alice told her.

'Honestly, I don't think you read enough true-crime novels in your formative years,' Bethany stated. She probably saw only his uncombed hair, his black eyeliner, his rumpled shirt.

Then they were at the science library, but Alice didn't want to go in. She headed back downtown and went into a department store instead. She bought a picnic basket.

When she got home, there was a message on her machine from Nellcott, which Alice found both cryptic and poetic. In other words, it was perfect.

He said, 'I'm with a friend at this place where you can get a hot dog fresh out of a bucket of steaming water. We're waiting for this guy to cut us a big piece of stainless steel but it's taking forever. There's a blond sixtyish lady beside us who overspent on her hairdo and who has a knack for bad accessorizing. I bet she'd go mad with jealousy if she turned her head and got a look at my sunglasses.'

Alice thought about calling Walker for some Nellcott advice. Sometimes when she called Walker, she got his mother. His mother would quickly say, 'He's not here,' and hang up before she could ask any more questions. His mom hated her, Alice was sure.

Sometimes she got Walker. He was making the perfect mixed tape to have sex by these days, which meant he was branching out into jazz.

He had made a schedule for himself. He was waking up an hour early each day just to listen to music before he had to face the day.

She had had a dream that Walker filled a Kleenex box with different women's underwear. When he sneezed, he whipped out a pair and blew into it.

This time Walker answered. He said, 'Alice, call me back in half an hour; I'm working on a screenplay.' He hung up. He was her mad genius at work.

She lit a candle. She painted her toenails blue. She called him back. 'There's this guy named Nellcott.'

'Call me back in an hour,' he said. 'The writing is going very well.'

William, Rally, Robert, Casey and Alice sat around the Film Society office. Rally sat on the desk. William stood. Robert got one of the orange chairs. Alice sat on a stack of phone books. Casey was leaning back on another orange chair, almost tipping over, which made Alice extremely nervous.

'Can anyone donate a couch?' William asked. When no one said anything, he started to freak out. 'You guys had to pick the most obscure Rolling Stones movie, didn't you? Nobody is going to come out to this.'

'Don't tell him it's in black and white,' Rally whispered to Alice.

There was going to be one special movie night when they were allowed to serve beer, and maybe even popcorn. It was going to be in the Student Union building instead of the Leacock Auditorium. Casey, the guy in charge of posters, picked out the Rolling Stones movie *Charlie Is My Darling* for that one.

'Relax, William, the artsy people will love it,' Rally said.

'What about *Gimme Shelter* or *Let's Spend the Night Together*?' William cried out.

Alice was thinking about the glasses she had on. She had watched one of her contact lenses go down the sink in the morning as she was putting it on. Her dad said he'd send her a new pair but it would take at least a week.

'You wear glasses?' Casey had asked.

Alice felt sick about it. Ugly, for sure. Her hair even seemed frizzier with glasses on. She would have to hide from Nellcott.

'All right, ideas for the film event,' William said. 'Alice, you're in charge of the popcorn.' He had to explain to her about petty cash. She had to buy the popcorn with her own money and then she'd be refunded in the basement of the Student Union building if she gave the people there her receipts.

'I was thinking,' Alice said. 'Instead of selling popcorn, we could sell Pop-Tarts.' What was going through her head? She didn't do drugs. Somehow, Pop-Tarts seemed quirky. Quirky was the way. 'Pop-Tarts will be cool. Pop-Tarts will create lifelong memories for everyone,' she said.

'You buy the Pop-Tarts,' William said.

Alice had been avoiding Nellcott because of her glasses, but he caught her on the street. She looked down immediately.

'Don't you feel like being together all the time?' he said.

'I lost my contacts.'

'I like the teacher look,' he said.

She rolled her eyes. She didn't.

'Go to school,' she said and pushed him lightly with an elbow. Then she remembered how the Rolling Stones movie night went and pulled him close. She was half joking, half crying in his arms about the Pop-Tart incident. There had been a good turnout for the movie but no one had bought a Pop-Tart.

'You could have told me to come out for the movie. The Rolling Stones are only my favourite band,' Nellcott said.

'You don't understand. It sounds stupid, but when I'm doing Film Society stuff, I have to concentrate. I don't want to have to pay attention to you.'

'I would have bought a Pop-Tart, darling.'

Her parents didn't even call each other *darling*. She wanted to stay with him forever because of the darling factor, the fact that he called her *darling*. That's all he had to do.

Nellcott followed Alice to the dorm and stopped.

'I thought we were going to have tea,' Alice said.

'Can you bring it out?'

Alice went in and got tea from the vending machine. She felt like she was sleepwalking.

Nellcott was sitting on the grass when she came out. He took the Styrofoam cup from her hand. He looked at the tea and said, 'I need to sit on the grass while I can. I get depressed in the winter when there's no grass to sit on.'

She took off her sandals and felt the grass under her feet. It was prickly. She lay down and looked at the sky. The dorm building jutted out diagonally and the sky was a puddle around it. She didn't move. She got scared telling herself, *This is what it must feel like to be dead*.

Nellcott ripped the cellophane off his cigarette package and drew out a cigarette.

'Why are you so fidgety?' she asked him.

'Hey,' he said, pointing a lit cigarette at her nose, 'if you're not nervous, you're dead.'

Then he kept looking at her. It made her nervous.

'I've been making fun of sandals my whole life and now I'm lovesick over a girl who wears sandals. A university girl.'

'Why aren't you in university again?' she asked. He looked older than her but not that much older.

'I took some courses but everything I need to know I can teach myself,' he said.

Alice looked at people going through the glass doors of the dorm and wondered what they thought of the two of them lying on the grass with no pillows or blankets.

She thought he was missing out, not being in school. She loved slumping in a chair and just listening to professors talk and talk about all this stuff she didn't know and all she had to do was listen and take a few notes. She loved it. Even now, she could hear her Children's Lit teacher go on about Peter Pan and the desire to be a child forever and how the pirates were really good characters.

She fell asleep beside Nellcott on the grass while he lit another cigarette and was a little restless but for the whole night stayed put.

When she woke up, it was morning. She felt a little crumpled and squinted around. Nellcott was still there staring at her.

'Wow, I've never slept outside before. Were we safe?' Students pushed open the glass doors and thudded out of the dorm.

Nellcott jumped up. 'I have to go to work.'

She didn't have Children's Lit until eleven. She walked Nellcott down the hill towards the campus and towards downtown. Her cotton T-shirt was a little rumpled, her jeans a little faded. Her flannel checked jacket had kept her warm. She could be a university student forever.

Nellcott walked by her side and her peripheral vision paid attention to him. He was loose under his shirt and a bit scattered, looking everywhere but at her. Alice stopped walking and looked at him until he told her what was up.

'I need to find someplace to tidy myself up before I go to work,' he said.

'Okay, well,' Alice said, looking around. There was Bethany's place close by on Durocher. Bethany lived off-campus with a friend. They stopped at a dep on the corner first. Nellcott bought a big carton of milk and some shaving supplies.

He walked into Bethany's living room with a pack of razor blades he had already ripped open. Bethany had heard only Alice's voice on the buzzer.

Bethany and her friends were these girls who taped TV shows and had giggly conversations, hands over their mouths. Now there was this wall of silence as Nellcott was in the bathroom behind a closed door. Alice and Bethany sat on the couch and waited, staring at the bathroom door. It felt to Alice like Bethany was never going to talk to her again. *He's only shaving*, Alice thought.

Bethany had said yes, he could use the bathroom, but later she said she didn't have a choice. She said, 'Great, Alice, now he knows where I live.'

When Alice went back up the dorm steps at the end of the day, Cricket and Allegra were there to ask her questions.

Cricket's head almost popped off her neck when she asked Alice, 'What were you doing sleeping outside? Who was the guy? Were you drunk?'

Alice had learned not to give out any personal information to anyone so she just nodded.

Allegra was mixing dry paints with water in Mason jars. She had at least ten paintbrushes pointing up in a Campbell's chicken noodle soup can. She was wearing a man's V-neck white under-shirt with splotches of paint on it and her men's pinstriped wool dark pants. She kissed the canvas to move around paint in the background a certain way and wiped off her lips with the back of her hand, keeping her eyes on the canvas the whole time.

Alice watched her like a little girl watches a ballerina twirling on a music box.

Allegra coloured her own hair blond. She cut her own bangs crazy short and jagged. She was impressed by things that glittered.

'Oh Allegra, sister, I found the perfect T-shirt for you,' Cricket announced. 'It says: "I'm not ADD. People just don't understand. Look, a sparkle!" Ha ha ha,' Cricket cackled.

But Cricket? Alice tried to stay out of Cricket's way.

Some rich guy really liked Cricket and Cricket just thought it was amusing. He called her from an airplane. Alice was impressed. Cricket was bored.

'He tried to take me to the mall, can you believe that? I refuse to go to the mall. I could stop breathing in a mall. Malls are so tacky,' Cricket said.

Those girls liked the little mom-and-pop shops on St. Laurent that looked like yard sales taken inside. They liked getting their clothes from the vintage-clothing stores on Mount Royal Street. When Alice checked it out, it was really just one street. She called it *used-clothing row* after Bob Dylan's song 'Desolation Row.' When she stepped inside the stores, the spaces were wall-to-wall cramped with clothes and she felt like she was always fighting with the racks when pulling out an item. The smells inside were musty and the lighting came from one, maybe two, red lampshades. The change rooms had velvet curtains that didn't fully cover the doorway so someone could always see in.

Allegra put away her paints and started down the hall with a quilted rucksack. Alice thought she was going to do laundry. Allegra asked Cricket for a couple of oranges and slipped them into her bag.

'Where are you going?' Alice asked her.

'I'm meeting this guy up on Mount Royal Cemetery. We're going to have tea and oranges by the tombstones.'

Allegra went out at night. Allegra was at bars. Allegra was on guest lists. Allegra was cooking for guys in their apartments.

Allegra went to a restaurant that sold magazines and all different types of candy.

Allegra went to a place that specialized in tea that looked like a haunted house and had wood floors that creaked.

Allegra had said, 'I cooked linguine and clams in a white-wine sauce for Jim, the owner of this club on St. Denis. It was a great night, only I had to stop him from using heroin.' Alice couldn't even imagine. She had never seen anyone do drugs. A couple of guys had shown up with red eyes and floppy heads in her Grade Twelve biology class but that was it.

Alice had met this guy, Jim. How he owned anything, let alone a club, was very perplexing. He veered towards the walls when he walked to Allegra's room. This guy was over forty. It was creepy.

Alice mentioned Allegra on the phone to Nellcott while she held her heart. A part of her thought Nellcott would like Allegra better than her if he met her. But a part of her thought they could all get along.

Alice was to meet Bethany in this young-people-run food place on St. Laurent, the Phoenix, that Rally had told her about. Rally liked the free coffee refills and the cute boys.

She had already dragged Nellcott once into the co-op's hodge-podge-lodge-decorated space. He had sneered at all the trendy-looking people in there. There was a carrot cake displayed under a plastic dome. The punk boy server had on a Mickey Mouse T-shirt like Emilio Estevez in *The Outsiders* and he had pink cheeks. He promised Alice she'd be able to taste the cream cheese in the icing. Nellcott looked like he was going to explode. 'What a load of crap,' he said. Alice had to get a piece to go, on a napkin, because Nellcott lasted only thirty seconds in the place before he said, 'I'll wait for you outside.' With Bethany, she was hoping for longer.

Rally had told Alice the kitchen staff got lettuce that was discarded at the back of Steinberg, the grocery store, so they wouldn't have to pay for lettuce. Alice wasn't going to tell Bethany that, though.

Alice waited for Bethany at a booth under art that displayed cereal in a plastic bag.

All the tables had brown sugar in square containers for the coffee that the place assumed you would order.

Bethany showed up and wiped the seat with a page from one of her notebooks before she sat down.

Whenever Alice saw Bethany, Alice compared her to Cricket and Allegra. It probably wasn't fair at all.

A guy with blue hair finally came and took their order. They both wanted veggie burritos. *There would be no lettuce in that,* Alice thought.

'So, how are things?' Bethany asked her. She had on a gold necklace and a gold bracelet, what seemed to Alice to be showcasing a lot of expensive jewellery.

'I could never wear a diamond engagement ring,' Alice said.

'What are you talking about?'

'Do you ever notice that everything you order in this town feels like breakfast?' Alice said, not wanting to explain herself.

'Honestly, that's because you don't wake up till the morning's almost over.'

It would be a miracle if Bethany agreed with Alice even one time.

'Our waiter just licked his fingers and then moved a burrito around on the plate,' Bethany said.

'No way,' Alice said, turning her head.

'Yeah,' Bethany said. 'You're getting that one.'

The veggie burritos came with mounds of hash browns on the side. The blue-haired guy plunked down the plates with a nonchalant expression. Alice watched him go behind the counter and turn up the music: Iggy Pop's 'I Wanna Be Your Dog.'

Bethany said, 'My roommate and I are thinking of going to Cancún for spring break.'

'I could never leave this town. Not even to go to Toronto. It's like when I'm here, I really want to conquer the town. I want to be a Montrealer.'

'But you're not,' Bethany said.

Alice slammed her right fist dramatically on the table. 'Where's your imagination, Bethany?'

'Are the lyrics of this song really "I wanna be your dog"?'

When Alice got to her room, she called Nellcott desperately and got his answering machine. When the beep went off to leave a message, she continued eating Cool Ranch Doritos without saying a word until there was a second beep and the message was over. Allegra had told her that those chips gave her psychedelic dreams if she ate them before she slept, and Alice believed her.

At ten-thirty that night, Bethany called Alice to say that she had been on the toilet for hours and that Alice was never to suggest a place to eat again.

Bethany had gotten in a fight with her roommate over cleanliness and had come to Alice's dorm room.

'Remind me never to room with you. I'm not the cleanest person either,' Alice said.

'Don't worry. It will never happen.' Bethany said, looking at the David Lynch photo with her head tilted to the side. It was weird for Alice to have someone in her space. She had wanted it; she had waited for it like a telephone wire waiting for birds to come. But with Bethany there, Alice worried if the place was clean enough.

'Go ahead and sleep in my bed,' Alice told her. 'I'm going to go study in the common room.'

Alice didn't know what she was doing when she opened her back-breaking knapsack and tried to get down to work. She took study breaks from her psychology textbook, crying, listening to Bob Dylan on her Walkman, wishing she were 'a topless dancer soon to be divorced' like in the 'Tangled Up in Blue' song.

Alice was finishing the first chapter of *The Wizard of Oz*. The cyclone had just hit. Bethany came running into the common room screaming.

'What is it?' Alice said.

'I was sleeping and all of a sudden there were rocks smashing into the window. Someone was attacking me in your room.' Bethany's hair was messed and her eyes were like a raccoon's.

'It was probably Nellcott. He does things like that.'

There was a pause as Bethany tried to comprehend that information. 'What? You're crazier than my roommate. I'm going home.'

Alice packed up her books and trudged back to her room. When she got there, Bethany was gone and Nellcott had made his way to her door.

Alice sat down on her bed. She tried to see her room as Nellcott was seeing it, for the first time.

The single bed, the blue sheets, the desk with the leaning tower of books stacked on it. A window that only cracked open so no one could jump out. A shelf with a popcorn maker. The tiniest fridge at the foot of her bed with nothing in it except a few ketchup packets. Walls that were so close to each other it reminded Alice of the trash-compactor scene in *Star Wars*.

Nellcott seemed to be looking only at her.

He had on a dark purple velvet jacket. She stroked his arm. She liked touching the velvet.

He had thick sideburns. Not Elvis big, but enough to look like a musician. He had a great head of hair. Black, almost navy. So thick and uncombed, about three inches all over – he probably cut it with dull scissors. She liked how a strand lay curled on his cheek. She knew he shaved every morning but now a little bit of black stubble was already poking through all along his jaw. She felt it when he started kissing her. It rubbed against her and hurt but she kept kissing back. He sort of rocked her as he was kissing her, then he stopped. He took off his shirt.

He lay on the bed with his head resting on her arm and waited. Then they kissed for a very long time. It was dark but there was a little light coming in from a street lamp. He took off her jeans. She let him but she was very tense.

'We can't have sex,' she finally said.

He did not understand and looked at her strangely.

'I'm still a virgin,' she said. She put her face in the pillow right after that.

'What?' he said.

She didn't answer.

'What were you doing all of high school?' he asked her.

Very funny, she thought. 'I was studying, okay? I wanted to go away to university more than anything else. I didn't want to get pregnant. I didn't want bad blood.'

'Have you seen my lighter?' he said, getting up.

She got up and turned on a light. She caught her reflection in the mirror on the wall. Her face was blotchy red where he had kissed her. 'Look what you've done to me,' she said.

He found his lighter, had a cigarette, put out his cigarette on the bottom of his boot and placed the butt on the windowsill. Like a true smoker, he had to have a smoke before making any kind of decision. Alice perched at the end of the bed in her underwear like a car ornament, wondering what he was going to decide about their relationship. It seemed beyond her control. It seemed like it could go fifty-fifty either away.

Then he started pacing around the bed like a shark. Layer by layer, he threw her comforter, blankets and sheet in the air.

'What is all this shit?' he said as blankets hit the floor.

'I only have one pillow,' she said. 'Should I buy another one?'

'Get in the bed,' he said as he turned off the light.

She hesitated.

'Don't worry,' he said. 'I'll restrain myself.'

He took the top sheet and whipped it up in the air above her. It was thin and light as it slowly fell on her body.

She woke up and Nellcott was gone. It didn't take her very long to see that he had drawn something on her thigh. *Nellcott was here* was inked with an arrow up her leg pointing to her crotch. She could not believe him and at the same time was slightly amused.

She was still thinking about being a virgin as she stood in line in the dorm's dining room at lunch. There were always two choices: meat or vegetarian.

'What's that?' She pointed at one of the meat dishes.

'Mystery meat,' the person in front of her said.

She ended up choosing vegetarian: a beans-and-rice dish with bits of corn, though vegetarian meals never filled her up.

She continued on down the line. They gave her an ice-cream ticket for dessert that was like the *Admit One* movie tickets they used at the Film Society. When the students were ready for dessert, they were supposed to take their tickets to the monitor in front of the freezer outside and scoop out the ice cream for themselves, two scoops maximum.

She filled up a glass with orange juice and carried her tray over to a bench where Allegra and Cricket were eating.

People around her were thirsty. They each had at least three glasses of pop on their trays: orange, yellow, black. She had grown up with no pop in the house. She didn't have one cavity.

The cafeteria was loud. She couldn't hear herself think. Alice couldn't say much. Especially when the girls in designer clothes started talking about soap operas. It seemed to be a useful way for a lot of them to relax.

Allegra and Cricket were eating vegetarian too. They were talking about the guys two tables over. They were about to leave.

'Do you want my ice-cream ticket?' Alice said, trying to make them stay longer. She never used it anyway. She didn't have much of a sweet tooth.

'All right.' Cricket snatched it up. 'Rocky road.'

'I want half,' Allegra said and they were gone. They got their ice-cream cones to go.

When Alice returned her cafeteria tray, Rally was there, taking it with brute force. She was hosing down trays. Alice hadn't known that Rally worked there. She felt bad that they made Rally wear this plastic shower cap on her head.

Alice stared. She felt bad that she didn't have to work like Rally and Nellcott. That she relied on her parents. That she would probably never be independent.

Rally didn't say anything. She went back to hosing down trays angrily. Alice stepped aside.

Later, Alice ruminated over Rally's shower cap as she walked back to the dorm through the falling leaves that seemed to die when she stepped on them. Rally walked by with a milk crate of records.

'What are you doing now?' Alice said.

'I DJ Friday nights.'

'You love the music. You need the pulse of the bass lines. You don't have time to waste sleeping,' Alice said.

'I need the money,' Rally said and kept walking.

The Film Society, though, Rally did that for free, Alice thought.

S he had not told Nellcott that Walker was coming.

'I can't see you this weekend,' she told him on the phone.

'School stuff?'

'Yeah.'

'You make me feel like a monk. You make me feel religious. One guy I know waited until he was married to have sex, but he was Muslim. Maybe I can do this.'

'That's reassuring.'

'Have a good weekend, darling.'

'You too.'

'You're not seeing someone else?' he asked.

'No, are you?'

'No.'

She had only ever seen Walker around the cafeteria in high school. He came in on the Greyhound bus with a backpack and his camera and real hiking boots. He bragged that he had already been hiking twice that year.

When they got to her dorm room, he looked for an ashtray and Alice was surprised she hadn't bought one yet since Nellcott smoked. Walker took out a red pack of DuMauriers. No one she knew smoked those. Nellcott smoked green Export A's and Allegra smoked Dunhills or Gauloises from France. She called them *Gauloilicious*. Walker said nothing about the David Lynch photo on the wall. She felt like she would never impress him.

He was eager to walk the streets. She'd promised to take him to the Word, a bookstore where they had many bookshelves and one in particular where they had books that were just a dollar.

Walker bought these heavy books by philosophers that she was not really interested in trying. She looked at the poetry chapbooks that local poets stapled together that were on display at the front of the store. The chapbooks had photographs on the covers that always looked great xeroxed. The poets wrote about being broke and in Montreal, drinking coffee out of tall glasses and kissing by garbage dumpsters.

Alice and Walker walked through the McGill ghetto and up Parc to Duluth. When they ran into street people, Walker would talk endlessly to them while she kept her hands in her pockets and fidgeted.

Walker took photos of paint peeling and other fine things he saw from his manual Nikon as they walked around. She wished she was that plastic bag caught in a tree as she waited for him to take the shot.

She thought Nellcott would appear from behind the next phone pole and catch her with a guy but he didn't.

Walker wouldn't take any glamour shots of Alice, though maybe her kneecap sometimes got in the frame or the side of her head which was all frizzy.

As their walking progressed, Alice came upon a white leather lounge lizard's shoe, one shoe, sticking up from a gate post, and it made her happy.

'Wow, that's a cool shot,' she said. 'Can you take a picture of that?'

Friday night, Walker and Alice slept in their clothes on her single dorm bed and she told herself they were like brother and sister.

Walker twisted and turned and she thought, *Please don't touch me.* He didn't and she finally fell asleep all crooked and tense.

In high school, Walker had one of those vanilla cloth bags that kids bought to write all over with black Magic Marker. He wrote stuff like *Jim Morrison is God*.

He crossed the street to smoke cigarettes with the rest of the smokers because there was no smoking on school property. When Alice went along, her eyes stared mostly at the street looking for her mom's blue Astro minivan to drive by and catch her with the smokers though she wasn't even smoking.

Walker would stop mid-sentence to climb a tree.

They both had Mr. Krackle for English. Mr. Krackle walked through the halls with John Lennon sunglasses and all his teaching materials in a cardboard box balanced on his hip.

Mr. Krackle had a poster of *The Sound of Music* in his classroom with black Magic Marker writing on it that said *This is the worst movie ever made.* When he covered Margaret Laurence's *The Stone Angel* and Steinbeck and Shakespeare even, Mr. Krackle always talked about movies, slipping in related examples here and there.

No matter how hard she tried, Alice could never make better than a B on a paper in his class. He graded everything out of five points. It drove everyone crazy. It didn't matter to Alice. She lived with it to hear Mr. Krackle's lectures.

She worried about Walker back then. At seventeen, he already had an ulcer. He chose this blond tough girl to be his everything. She smoked cigarettes too and they were always searching through each other's backpacks. This girl would slap Walker on the forehead out of nowhere from time to time, which only gave him this goofy smile. She didn't talk to him anymore after high school. Something had happened.

When she woke up, Alice noticed that Walker had big pillowy lips. Pretty soon, Walker's eyelids went up and he was looking back at her.

'Mr. Krackle always liked you better than me,' she said. 'You think it was 'cause I'm a girl?'

'What are you talking about?'

'Well, he'd nod to you in the hallways, and he gave you A's on your papers. And he didn't turn you in to the principal though he must have known you were the one who spray-painted *Jim Morrison is God* in the hallway.'

'Yeah, he gave me a pretty good recommendation for Ryerson too.'

'So, why didn't he like me?'

'I don't know.'

She got up and stomped around a bit. She ripped the David Lynch photo off her wall and tossed it in the trash bin under her desk. 'So, what do you want to do today?' she asked Walker. She wanted him to say, 'Get you a new poster for your wall.' But he didn't.

'I wanna shoot some more photos,' he said.

She got her bathroom bucket with her toothpaste and toothbrush and walked out.

Saturday night, Walker bought a bottle of red wine at the depanneur and they walked over to Prince Arthur Street where it turned to cobblestone. The street was closed off to cars. All the restaurants there had a bring-your-own-wine policy – they couldn't sell it but you could bring it and they would open it for you and serve it – and all the restaurants had outdoor seating. It was still warm enough to be outside.

Walker talked about his sex life as she watched waiters in their starched white uniforms perfectly balance glasses of wine.

She wondered how long she and Walker would be friends. Did he really like her and why? She didn't ask him these questions, but she wondered.

'I'm gonna move to L.A. when I graduate,' he said. 'I'm gonna be in bed with a bunch of phones.'

When they got back to the dorm they tumbled on the bed and just lay there, full from the wine and chicken kebabs and rice. Allegra walked by in a silk kimono. Walker sat up and invited her in to see the philosophy books he had bought. Alice got bored and went to the bathroom. Allegra was gone when she got back and so was Walker.

Alice fell back onto the bed in her clothes and felt like a chalk drawing of a dead person that the police would make. She was that tired.

Alice walked into Allegra's room the next day looking for signs of Walker but there were none. There were no signs that any guy had ever been there. Alice sprawled on the floor next to Allegra with her head on one of Allegra's big purple throw pillows.

Allegra was painting. Her canvases were always life-size and her figures were always pale so you could see the background right through their skin. Often she would paint in veins or bones. She had a nervous hand but steady eyes.

Allegra said, 'I think in your films you should have women who walk around in trench coats.'

'My films?' Alice said.

'Aren't you in the Film Society for a reason?'

'I don't think making films is going to happen to someone like me.'

'And always have the women walk out on the men in the restaurant scenes and don't ever make a film without a rain scene.'

'Okay,' Alice said.

Allegra lifted her paintbrush and put a little purple in her green background.

'How did you know to do that?' Alice asked her.

'I didn't *know* – I just wanted to and then it's done.' She sighed and Alice assumed her friend was getting tired of her. 'There's nothing wrong with doing what you want to do.'

Allegra didn't feel like going to dinner. She was going to window-shop on St. Catherine Street and Alice asked her if she could come.

'I guess,' Allegra said.

'Did you like my friend Walker?' Alice asked her on the street with the cold wind and the pavement and the black skinny trees.

'He was okay.'

When they walked past Pier One Imports, a store where newly married people bought dishes and placemats, Allegra stopped and stared at the windows like she was star-struck. She went in and Alice followed her, walking around the store with her big oversized knapsack, trying not to bump into any of the dish displays or the wineglasses that were stacked in a pyramid.

Allegra picked out a mug that had swirls down the inside. 'I like to go in and pick out my favourite mug of the day and sometimes I buy one.' That explained the assortment of mugs Allegra had on her bookshelf.

Alice said, 'And when you're mad at a guy, you shove your mugs out the window crack and watch them smash on the pavement below.'

'It's not just guys,' Allegra said. 'One day, you'll piss me off too.'

Alice was still unnerved about the possibility of Allegra being mad at her as they drank pints of draft at the Bifteck.

An older guy in an expensive black dishevelled suit with a woman on his arm who looked like she probably worked in the sex trade walked towards them. The man froze at the sight of Allegra.

'Hi, Jim,' Allegra said.

'I'll go look for Chris at the bar,' his woman said to him.

'She means nothing to me,' Jim said under his breath when the woman was out of sight. 'I think about you every day.' He seemed transfixed.

Unbelievable, Alice thought.

'Sure, Jim,' Allegra said.

His woman came back from the bar. 'Come on, Jim. He's not here,' she said and he reluctantly followed. 'We're getting married,' she yelled back at Allegra.

'Is that true?' Alice said.

'Doesn't matter.'

'Isn't he the club owner who does heroin?'

Allegra answered by downing her pint of beer in one shot.

A guy with a goatee came over to talk to Allegra and the subject was closed. He used his cigarette to point out the things he was lecturing about. She stole the cigarette right out of his hand and took a long draw off it from the side of her mouth.

Allegra had this big smile on her face. 'He's a lecturer,' Allegra whispered in Alice's ear. She turned his cigarette into a magic wand.

'What's your name?' he asked Allegra.

'Petunia,' she said.

The beer Alice was drinking shot out of her nose.

Nellcott was working that night which was too bad because Alice thought maybe he could finally meet Allegra.

Alice was starting to miss him when they weren't together. That day she had bought a blue glass ashtray for him at Pier One when Allegra wasn't looking.

Nellcott had bought an old boxy brown car with a friend at work. It made chugging and gagging noises. *Who splits a car payment with a friend?* Alice thought. Nellcott picked her up at the dorm.

'It would be fine if it wasn't brown,' Nellcott said about the car.

His right leg jerked on the accelerator. She noticed the car had a stick shift. She had never learned to drive one of those and was impressed.

He let the car rev up and then went for the radio. When he turned the knob, it sounded like someone was being electrocuted.

'The radio's crap, anyway,' he said and turned it off.

When Nellcott drove, he had his own style. He looked straight ahead with his right arm straight out and his right hand gripping the top of the wheel. When she looked at him, he could always tell and he'd look over at her. Every time.

When she looked down between her feet, she saw a small hole in the floor of the car. The pavement was whizzing by.

They were on their way to an area of town she had never been to before. He told her someone had been mugged there recently, his throat slit.

With one foot in the door, she saw everything. The dried-up spaghetti in the pot on the stove that looked like angel hair. The half melon scraped out and used as an ashtray, the cabinets crowned with empty liquor bottles and the empty beer bottles stacked in the corner.

'Keep your shoes on,' Nellcott said.

Nellcott pried Alice's knapsack off her shoulders and threw it in a closet. He kicked it a few times until the closet door could completely shut.

Nellcott led her past the kitchen and down a hallway to a living room situation. There was a record player. Records were stacked all around. They probably weren't all Nellcott's, but he knew his way around. There were three old couches that had probably been dragged in from the street. Alice sat on the brown corduroy one.

A guy came down the stairs, his arm reaching way ahead for the banister, his workboots making a tap dance on the wooden stairs.

He was just as skinny as Nellcott. He had on tight jeans and he had dirty blond hair that looked soft and came past his ears a little. He had a big friendly grin on his face.

He had no shirt on and shaving cream on half his face and he kissed her on both sides of the mouth like French people do.

Nellcott was not the type to shake hands or kiss cheeks when meeting someone. Maybe he would nod at you with locked, staring eyes. He looked tough and scared people away.

The shaving cream felt like whipped cream on her cheek and she left it on for a second before laughing and wiping it off with the back of her hand and then rubbing it into her skin. Nellcott looked on with his mouth open.

'What's your name?' Nellcott's roommate asked her. He had a deep voice.

'Petunia,' she said.

'Don't pull that shit,' Nellcott said.

Alice looked down at her sandals.

'I'm Gregory,' he said.

'Alice,' she said.

'Nice to meet you, Alice. I've got to get to the hospital.' He leaped back up the stairs. When he left a few minutes later, he had a bag over his shoulder and he tossed his keys up in the air and caught them on his way out the door.

'Why's he going to the hospital?' Alice asked.

'He works there as an orderly,' Nellcott said.

She tried to picture Gregory cleaning toilets.

'I guess I can make you some tea,' Nellcott said and went back to the kitchen.

The kitchen table was a stolen picnic table with girls' names carved on it. Alice ran her fingers over names like Louisa-Marie and Jeannette.

'Are these your previous girlfriends?' she asked.

'No.' Nellcott was banging around the kitchen trying to find things. His boots were loud too. She was sure they would scare the animals if he had any.

'I lived with a girl for three years,' Nellcott said. He was sponging off the counter with a piece of bread. She winced at the colour it was turning. 'A dancer. We lived in the apartment right under my mom. I drove the girl crazy.'

'Three years. You must be in love with her still.'

He didn't answer.

'How many times have you had sex?' she asked him.

'I can't answer that question. Many times.' He used an old beer bottle with some beer still in the bottom to put out his cigarette.

'Have you had sex with anyone who went to my university?'

'Probably.' He was opening and closing cupboards, having trouble finding the tea, and then he found some.

Nellcott went out to the living room to play another record. The sound floated by scratchy and it sounded like rain. Alice couldn't think of the last time she had heard a record playing.

They did not have any mugs. He prepared the tea in Mason jars where you could see the tea catching the light of the room and she liked it that way.

He gave her one of the jars and she asked him, 'You haven't already had sex with Allegra and are not telling me?'

'I've been with Rally.'

'You had sex with Rally from the Film Society?'

'One time. After that she started throwing things at me.'

Alice could see them going at it up against a wall. She made a disgusted face. 'Where did you have sex?'

'In a hallway at a party.' She could see it happening right then. He sat up on the counter by the sink. 'Let me show you my room,' he said, jumping back down.

As they passed Gregory's room, she saw a poster of Jim Morrison and she was proud that she could recognize it. It was the one with his bare chest and red beaded necklace.

Nellcott's room was sparse. The walls were yellowish all over. The room was mostly filled with a bed. Alice looked at the bed – it was as high as her waist.

'I built this bed with my own hands,' Nellcott said.

There was no place to sit except the bed.

Bread-and-butter plates were scattered around and used as ashtrays. An acoustic guitar leaned against the wall. There were no framed photos on display. Some milk crates were arranged on their sides for shelving. There was a bedsheet covering the window. There was a phonebook that looked like it had been left out in the rain.

A laminated backstage pass hung on his closet door with a picture of a sexy full-bodied naked woman on it.

'Let's hear about your boyfriends,' he said.

'I never had a real boyfriend,' she said. 'I had a crush in high school, an all-consuming crush, on the same guy for three years. The only person who knew about it was Bethany and she's kept my secret to this day.'

'What kind of friend is that?' he said.

He invited her to stay the night. She loved sleepovers. She liked sleeping in different spaces. For her, it was like slipping into different lives. She said okay.

She would have to sleep with her contacts in and wake up with sticky eyes. She had not brought pyjamas and didn't even think of sleeping naked. She looked in Nellcott's dresser for something to wear. She pulled out pyjamas that were pink with red stripes.

Nellcott moaned. 'My dad gave me those for Christmas.'

'You could wear these; you're in touch with your feminine side. Aren't you?'

'Yeah, but I'm not going to wear them.'

Because they were a gift? Alice wondered what someone was supposed to get Nellcott as a gift. He seemed impossible to shop for.

Under the pyjamas in the drawer, there was a card with a big cartoon Santa with sunglasses giving the peace sign. Inside it said:

> *Dear Nellcott,*
> *Remember that not all of us in the straight world think straight. We just act it and do our own thing anyway.*
> *Love always,*
> *Dad xxx*

When she looked up, Nellcott was staring at her like *What are you doing?*

'Sorry,' she said, putting the card back in the drawer.

When she got in his tall bed and lay down it was so high that she felt like the princess and the pea, only it was coins that were under the mattress.

He let her spoon him but it was never the other way around. She was learning to rely on his smell. Up close, he always smelt like fresh laundry which overpowered the cigarette smell that hung in the air.

When she looked down, his boots were poking out from under the sheets.

At the next Film Society meeting, Alice couldn't help staring at Rally. Rally looked at Alice and stuck her nose back in her work.

'What are you doing?' Alice asked.

'I'm researching my honours thesis on the theory of the sublime.'

Alice had no idea what that meant but was self-conscious about asking anyone more than one question at a time.

Rally had brewed her coffee herself that morning and was now sipping it from a silver carry-it-with-you mug. She had two thin braids, one going down each side of her face, like Kelly Lynch in *Drugstore Cowboy*, and her gloves had the finger tops cut off, probably on purpose.

Casey was pulling a Pop-Tart wrapper down like a banana peel. 'I think strawberry is still my favourite,' he said. The Pop-Tarts were all stacked on the top shelf of the metal cabinet. They had more Pop-Tarts than paper for flyers.

'Hey,' Alice said to Rally after the meeting. 'Why didn't you tell me you had sex with Nellcott, my boyfriend?'

She already had her messenger bag slung over her shoulder and was out the door. 'I did. Oh, that's right. I did.'

Alice thought that the more words Rally could say about him, the more he belonged to Rally and not to her.

'Can you tell me more about him?'

'You haven't had sex yet, have you?'

Alice let the question hang in the air like a rainstorm.

Alice wanted to go for a drink with her. They went to a local pub where beer was supposed to be recycled.

'What does that mean?' Alice asked.

Rally told her with limited patience, 'It means if someone doesn't finish their pitcher of beer, we end up getting it. Order something that comes in a bottle.' She took out her pack of cigarettes. She offered Alice one and Alice accepted. Alice knew she would never have smoked with Nellcott. She didn't want to encourage his bad habits, but with Rally it was sort of fun.

'Do you like any of the guys in the Film Society?' Alice asked.

'No, I see them too much. I have a crush on a flaky sort of comic-artist guy.'

'Are you looking for a boyfriend?'

'I have a policy that I only consider having a boyfriend in January so February turns out okay. I've declared February sexual-frustration month.'

'Doesn't it kill you when it's over with a guy?'

'I'd rather give a guy my body than my time.' Rally looked up at the big-screen TVs in the place. A Tom Petty video that was on the screen was re-enacting *Alice in Wonderland*. Alice's body was a cake and Tom Petty was the Mad Hatter, cutting it up and giving it to people.

'How did we end up in a sports bar?' Alice asked her.

'They have cheap wings,' Rally said.

Rally talked about her friends and their Sunday brunches and potluck dinners. She told Alice about putting a salad together the best way, using olive oil and balsamic vinegar.

'But never let a guy near you when you're making chili,' she said. 'They'll just want to add ketchup or beer.'

'Okay,' Alice said, feeling like she should be taking notes.

Rally said that she wanted to go home and take a long leisurely bath and read the book-of-the-month book that her mom had sent her. Alice lived too much in her mind to take all that time having a bath. She couldn't remember the last time she had had one.

'I have nightmares about eating peanut-butter sandwiches for the rest of my life,' Rally said.

'I have nightmares about doing laundry,' Alice said. In the dorm there was only one washer and dryer for the whole building. Alice felt like it was never her turn. And once she put her stuff in the washer she couldn't leave or else someone would dump her wet stuff on the floor.

'I've found that I can wait longer to do my laundry if I turn my underwear inside out and wear it that way too,' Rally told her.

Alice thought that was probably the best university survival tip she had heard yet.

But with sex – with sex she was still clueless, though somebody sometime somewhere told her it was just another way of dancing with someone.

Alice and Nellcott were walking through the rugby field in the centre of campus and she leaned back. He was supposed to hold her up like in a tango.

'Okay, I'm doing the dip now,' she'd say.

'So, the guy you had a crush on for three years, what was his favourite band?' Nellcott asked her.

'The Police.'

'I guess that's not so bad.'

She leaned back and he held her with his arm, his other hand holding hers, and he leaned over and put his face right in front of hers and asked, 'If you saw him right now, would you still have a crush on him?'

'Yes.'

He let go of her and her butt smacked the grass.

'Ow. I can't believe you did that.'

'Believe it.'

'I will always have a crush on my crush. I will always love the feelings I had on my first crush, to know that I could have those feelings.'

'Do you have those feelings for me?' he ventured.

'I can't answer that,' she said, getting up. She was secretive and scared. But she thought of him as the part of her she was missing, the part she wished she had.

He looked sad but he offered her his hand and they kept walking.

The next time Alice went over to Nellcott's, Gregory's girlfriend, Shelley, was over. Shelley had green eyes and long, straight honey-blond hair. She had the reddest lips and wore a beat-up army jacket over an Indian-print dress and combat boots. She had a bulldozer personality.

She had a purse too. Alice had a whole bunch of things stuffed in her front jean pockets that made a big bulge in her pants almost like a guy.

Gregory, Shelley and Nellcott talked about Thursdays at Purple Haze and Friday folk nights at Concordia University and Saturday nights at Double Deuce.

They were passing around a joint.

When it came around to Alice she just shook her head.

'Where are you from?' Shelley asked her.

'Toronto.'

'You mean Trauma, Ontario,' Gregory said, like he'd been busted there once.

Shelley said to Nellcott, 'I'm taking Gregory to Paris this New Year's, Nelly. I'm making great tips at Lola's.' *Nelly*? Alice had never thought of calling him that.

'What are you kids doing tonight?' Gregory asked.

'We're going to hang out here,' Nellcott said.

'Well, we'll be down the street.' *Down the street* was their local bar. They liked it even though mostly old men frequented the place. The bar sold one-dollar hot dogs and, of course, poutine, the Quebecois dish of French fries with gravy and melted cheese curds on top.

'Have you ever done acid?' Nellcott said after they left.

'No.'

'I think you and I should do acid sometime.'

'I don't think so.'

'We'll see.'

No, we won't, Alice thought. He was exhausting.

'Cigarette?'

'No.'

Alice went over to the record player. She put on some Joni Mitchell. 'Aghh!' Nellcott put his hands over his ears. 'That's not mine, that's Gregory's, and he probably only likes it 'cause of Shelley.'

She tried again. She went over to another corner of the room and pulled out some David Bowie.

'I feel like dancing,' Alice said when the guitar started its first few strums.

'I don't dance,' he said.

She looked at him, puzzled. The music went on and then Nellcott started pointing his cigarette like a piece of chalk. 'This is the part of the song that kills it for me. It's like he's sucking on popsicles.'

She never knew what he was going to say. He was like a movie with breakout dialogue. *You dance by inhaling on your cigarette*, she thought.

When Nellcott threw off his coat, then his shirt, then his silk scarf, it looked like splotches of different-coloured paint splattering on the floor.

He kissed her and then opened her mouth and kissed her entire mouth. The hair on his face was coarse and prickly again and her face turned red and sore. She was still not at the point where she felt she could tell him to shave.

Alice was naked. It was odd for her. He told her she was beautiful.

He had broad shoulders and strong arms and she lay in the crook of his neck and then on his chest.

After kissing her intensely, he would lie so tense and rigid. He had stopped trying for more. She was surprised that he could be the least bit scared of her.

She liked to put her index finger in the place where his belly button dropped.

He lit a match and she could hear the paper of his cigarette burn when he inhaled.

'Tell me a story,' she said. 'So I can sleep.'

'What, did your parents read to you when you were a kid?'

'Yeah.' This was true. Her parents used to take her to the Fairview Library, which had a Noah's Ark for children to read in, when she was little. The ark had had tons of stuffed animals and books in plastic see-through wrapping that crackled when you opened them.

She turned over on her side facing away from him, ready to sleep, hoping not to offend him. Their butts touched for a brief moment. Then Nellcott flopped around like a fish out of water.

Cars were driving by. She loved the part where the light from the headlights drifted above her head from one side of the ceiling to the other. Nellcott went downstairs to the kitchen with a screwdriver and took apart the toaster to see what was inside.

She was going over to Nellcott's on the bus more often and when she'd get there she would usually head straight to the brown corduroy sofa exhausted and hinting for Nellcott to feed her. She was getting used to his Kraft Dinner, his scrambled-egg sandwiches and his tuna-fish surprise.

She knew things about him now, like the fact that he washed his underwear every night in the sink. He prided himself on never wearing ripped jeans. He had been through a hundred drunken mishaps and never had had to wear a cast.

Alice would often bring a book to read for pleasure – not that she officially had the time. She was reading *Hammer of the Gods* about Led Zeppelin. Her eyes would widen when Jimmy Page fell in love with fourteen-year-old girls and then dumped them. This was not making her want to have sex.

Nellcot was reading *The Gathering Storm* by Winston Churchill. He liked anything that had to do with war. She liked everything on hippies.

She was nineteen and Nellcott was twenty-three.

Her parents had a five-year difference between them and they were still together. They had met when her father dropped a pen and they both bent down to pick it up and her father broke her mother's nose.

Alice had always loved looking at her parents' wedding album. The last photo was the best. Her parents had slipped out of their formal wedding attire and were off to the honeymoon. It was a photo of them holding hands on the stairs and looking over their shoulders at the camera. Her mom with her long ironed hair had on a pink suede suit and high leather boots. Her dad had long sideburns. They were rescuing each other from their crazy mothers. When Alice's mom and dad had gotten together, the world had shifted around them.

Nellcott's parents were divorced. He told her he remembered this big argument between them when he was two and eating a pear.

'Are we going to last?' Alice had asked Nellcott a couple of times now.

He always said, 'Stick around, darling.'

She told him the story about how when her parents first dated, all they could afford on the menu was French onion soup. So Nellcott told her he would take her out for a French onion soup date, no problem. Only, when she put a spoonful of gooey Swiss cheese in her mouth it lodged in the back of her throat and she thought she was going to choke to death.

One night at the Film Society they showed John Cassavetes' *Husbands*. Alice's jaw almost fell off. The three husbands in the movie had a strong camaraderie. They behaved badly when they went overseas. But they were real and passionate about life.

There was this one scene where John Cassavetes' character calls his wife from a pay phone and says to her, 'You're my sweet-potato pie.'

Alice stepped out of that movie like stepping out of a really warm shower.

Later, she asked Nellcott if he liked sweet-potato pie.

'No,' he said.

'Can you call me your sweet-potato pie? That would be really cool.'

'I don't like sweet potatoes.'

'You don't have to like sweet potatoes.'

He rubbed his long fingers a few times through his scarecrow hair, almost pulling some of it out. He said, 'Why don't I just call you *darling*?'

She looked down. A part of her felt like breaking up with him right then. But soon he was flitting around doing something else. She liked watching him move around a room, and the moment passed.

Alice received an invitation under her door. It was a photograph of a stately house in the country with white pillars and many windows and trees in front. On the back was written *An invitation to a social gathering* and then the time, date and place. Beside the word *place* was written *the den of iniquity (pictured on the reverse)*. Nellcott and Gregory were having a party.

When Alice asked Nellcott over the phone who was coming, he told her, 'The key to feeling popular is to buy yourself a really small address book.'

Friday night she was supposed to go out with Bethany.

She was nervous. She was excited. She didn't care.

She'd dress in something revealing. She was bold when it came to that. She was a tease.

She broke the news of the party to Bethany. Bethany refused to go, so she asked Allegra, who agreed.

'You're finally going to meet Nellcott,' Alice said, jumping up and down.

'Calm down,' Allegra said.

'I don't have anything to wear.'

Allegra took Alice on the metro to Pie-IX station and they went to Value Village where they could get second-hand clothes cheap. Allegra was a pro. Alice wheeled the shopping cart while Allegra filled it with satin jackets and decadent ashtrays and lamps that had shades with fringes. She picked out a pair of little girl's shoes to remind her of her childhood and fought with a punk girl with pigtails over a blouse with a sewn-in tie.

After about an hour, Allegra led Alice to the fitting rooms in the back. They modelled for each other. Most of the choices fit funny, so when something worked it was extra-exciting.

When they got to the party they had swinging purses and lace gloves and Allegra swayed near Alice's face to make Alice check her breath. It smelled like a snowdrift.

Inside, Alice realized they were supposed to bring their own beer: a case per person seemed to be the going ratio.

'We don't need to buy beer,' Allegra said when Alice brought it up. 'That's what guys are for.'

Nellcott handed them two blonds – what the light beer was called – and Allegra kissed him on the lips for it. Alice cringed.

Alice was wearing a cream-coloured lace top that she had seen Courtney Love wear in a band photo. She also wore red lipstick, a black velvet skirt and fishnet stockings. Her mother's mouth would drop open in horror if she saw Alice made up that way. Alice hadn't been allowed to wear makeup in high school. Alice whispered in Nellcott's ear, 'Are you going to take a photo of me? I won't always be able to dress like this.' And Nellcott said, 'Why the hell not?' She smiled at the floor.

Nellcott was wearing jeans and a white T-shirt that showed his body and a red Moroccan scarf around his neck. He offered Alice his arm and she took it until he left her to get more beer.

Alice hadn't washed her hair in two days and she found it looked better: more clumpy and less frizzy. The pillows on her bed must have straightened it as she slept.

Alice didn't recognize anyone except Nellcott and Gregory and Shelley and, of course, Allegra. People were greeting each other by kissing twice, once on each cheek, the Montreal way.

Alice and Allegra grabbed a spot on the floor by some records and watched the people around them who were mostly wearing black under black leather jackets and who already seemed to be drunk.

Gregory came by and hugged her and said, 'Hi, Alice.' His eyes were sliding off to the side but Alice was grateful for the greeting. So many people's eyes at school were cold and judgmental and oh so serious.

'I think the floor is sticky,' Alice said and popped back up. The couches were all taken.

Nellcott seemed to be talking to a lot of different people; Alice liked watching him across the room. When she saw him drink out of someone else's beer bottle, she wondered about germs but quickly stopped herself.

Alice went to the bathroom. Shelley was waiting in line too.

'Who's your friend?' Shelley asked her.

'Allegra. She's in the room beside me at my dorm.'

'She is permanently pouting.'

Alice looked at her friend. Allegra was sitting in some guy's lap and grabbing the cigarette out of his lips. 'She's a really good artist,' Alice said with pride.

'She looks like a dead dolly.'

Alice shrugged her shoulders.

'If she touches Gregory, I'm going to punch her in the nose,' Shelley said.

When Alice got back to Allegra, Allegra was standing up.

'What are you doing?' Alice said.

'Let's go.'

'Hi,' Nellcott said, immediately by their side. 'You guys can't be leaving, it's only eleven. Parties don't really get started until now.'

'I'm bored,' Allegra said.

'Hey, Nellcott, this is Allegra. Remember, I was telling you about her art?' Alice said.

'What's the problem? Parties aren't like this in Toronto? I bet in Toronto, the first thing people ask each other is, "What do you do for a living?"'

'Don't insult Toronto,' Allegra said. 'You know your girl-friend's from there. Why would you do that?'

'You want me to lie?'

'I want you to get out of my way. We're going. I have to study.'

'What? On a Friday night?'

'I have a mid-term Monday in Art History. I want a 4.0 GPA.'

'What's a GPA?'

'Grade Point Average,' she said like he was deaf.

'Don't you want a 10.0?'

'Let's go, Alice.'

'What can they teach you in school anyway? Really?' Nellcott was saying this pretty close to Allegra's face. 'You should get a job and see what it's like. Maybe you'll learn some economics.'

'Don't talk to me like that. My mom worked at Burger King.'

'My mom worked at McDonald's.'

'Okay, you guys want a beer?' Gregory held up two bottles in front of them.

Allegra led Alice outside with Nellcott trailing close behind.

'I'm pretty tired anyway,' Alice said to him.

'Here's a cab,' Allegra said.

Nellcott followed them outside with no coat and climbed on the hood of the cab, begging them to stay.

'Get off my cab.' The driver was furious, waving his arm out the window.

'Come on, Alice. Get out of the car,' Nellcott said.

'Stay in the car,' Allegra said to Alice, ordering the driver, 'Just go.'

When Nellcott jumped down to go up to the cab window, the driver took off.

Alice kept quiet as Allegra called him a freak and an asshole.

Allegra asked her, 'How can you go out with him? He is so rude. He doesn't even know me. He has no right to tell me to get a job.'

'I'm so sorry,' Alice said.

Dance music throbbed in the cab. The cab driver kept turning around to them in the back seat, asking them what kind of drugs they were on as he zoomed down Montreal's one-way streets. Alice stayed quiet as Allegra answered, 'Crack.'

As the cab driver drove, Alice knew she liked Nellcott, but she thought they might be doomed.

When they got to their dorm, Allegra went into her room and shut the door in Alice's face.

There were three long messages on Alice's answering machine from Nellcott describing the party in great detail like a reporter, telling her everything she was missing and saying that he wished she were there.

If she were Nellcott, she would turn right around and jump in a cab and go back there. But she was so tired, the kind of tired where she could feel the blankets on her before she got under them. She slipped her feet under the covers and then the rest of her and she was gone.

In the morning she listened to her messages again. She hadn't been dreaming. There was a message from her mom. 'It's eleven-thirty in the night, why are you not there? Where are you? Your dad and I are coming up to visit you on Thanksgiving.'

Alice's stomach dropped. She had known a visit from her parents was coming but she didn't know how to be calm about it. Would she have to introduce them to Nellcott? She didn't want to. Her parents could put her back in her pink and green bedroom in their house and stick her with a curfew.

When Alice walked around campus in the cool breezes and the fall chill, she felt really lonely, but she could think about her dad. Before Alice was born, her dad had been her age and he had wandered around the very same campus.

She liked the old buildings of the campus, the tall black iron gates that guarded some of the entrances, the park in the centre where the architecture students would try to level some traffic-light-yellow tripod-like machines. The Arts Building steps, where people hung out to see and be seen. The main floor of the Redpath Library, which had a section called *the fishbowl* because it was enclosed with glass and had comfy chairs where you could read. The campus was enchanting, even if you were failing Abnormal Psychology and you were hanging out with a guy your parents would be scared of and your friends already were.

Walking down the path that led out the campus through the side gates there was a one-way traffic sign. Someone had written in the white arrow the word *Reality*. Alice didn't think she could make it in the real world; she had four years to put it off.

When her parents came, she didn't tell Nellcott about it.

They sat her down at the hotel restaurant, one on either side of her. There were linen tablecloths and high-priced items and no smoking anywhere.

She started by ordering tea.

'You're drinking tea now? Don't you know that will stain your teeth? Think of all the money we've spent on those teeth,' her mother said.

Alice flashed a toothy smile.

The waiter was beside her offering an open tea chest with different teas sectioned off with red velvet compartments. There were about twelve different kinds. Time stood still. She couldn't make a decision.

She pointed to one wrapped in shiny yellow paper.

Her mother said, 'So, Granny's been asking if you're wearing the pearls she got you for your birthday. Are you wearing them?'

'Mom, no one my age wears pearls,' Alice said. She was trying to think where she'd put them.

Then her dad said, 'Grandma wants to know if you're dating arts students because she says arts students belong on the end of a rope.'

'No, no arts students,' Alice proudly reported.

The waiter placed a metal teapot in front of Alice. Alice's hand started shaking as she poured out her tea from the stainless-steel teapot into a china cup.

'So, everyone at this table who's had sex before raise their hand,' her dad said. Her parents' hands shot up. She couldn't believe them.

'I'm not telling you if I've had sex.' Her parents looked at each other then brought down their hands. She hadn't even had sex yet.

Alice started crying. The waiter didn't know how long it was going to last and if he should wait until she was done.

'We just want you to do your best and to be happy,' her mom said as Alice's face got puffier.

'Grandma just wants to know if you are doing the right things to further yourself. Are you furthering yourself?' her dad asked, popping his eyes out.

'I'm failing Abnormal Psychology,' Alice said. She had missed the withdrawal date to get out of the course before it counted in her GPA. She felt so stupid.

Her parents said that was all right. Her dad said, 'So you fail a course. You're still going to the university I went to.'

Alice was still crying. 'And I'm seeing someone I really like.'

'Well, then, why would you be crying?' her mother said.

'You won't like him.'

'Does Bethany like him?' her mother asked.

'I like him!' Alice said emphatically.

Her parents grew very silent. Her dad was fidgeting with the silverware on his napkin and her mother was looking down at her empty plate.

'What do you have in common with this boy?'

'Music.'

'That's not enough to base a relationship on.'

'Maybe I should get a job.'

'You are not getting a job,' her mother said, like it was a dirty thing. 'Your job is to focus on your studies.'

'Stay away from boys,' her dad said. 'They will only rape you and leave you with nothing.'

Her parents looked back and forth at each other and at Alice.

Alice felt like running, like calling Nellcott, but he would somehow find out where they were and show up at their table like a spilt drink.

Her mother had brought two pies and a cooked chicken for Alice's three-pop-can fridge. As her mom waited by the dorm's elevator downstairs, Alice took off running up the stairs. 'I'll meet you up there,' Alice said. Alice got to her room first and stashed the blue glass ashtray at the back of her sweater drawer, ashes and all. Then she straightened her comforter as best she could and sat down on the bed, crossing her legs.

Her mother was soon at her door, sniffing the air as she walked in. She noticed the popcorn maker sitting innocently on the shelf.

'This is not the popcorn maker I gave you for university,' her mother said.

'I know.'

'So where is the one I gave you?'

'They had a movie night here at the dorm and went around asking for popcorn makers and they saw mine and took it. Someone brought this one back. I really didn't want to go to every room asking if they had my popcorn maker.'

'Alice, your popcorn maker was better.'

Alice looked at the popcorn maker.

'This popcorn maker is called Pop It,' her mother said. 'It weighs half as much as yours and it doesn't have that long plastic guide to lead the popcorn into the bowl. I can't even think of the mess it would make; it's too much. You try to get the best for your kids and they give it away.'

Alice was stunned. She didn't know what to say. And even if she had known what to say she wouldn't have said it, because she had to hold her tongue around her mother.

Why did her battles in life have to be about popcorn makers?

'Where is Dad anyway?' Alice asked.

'He wanted to give us some mother-daughter time. He's at the hotel swimming.' That was her dad. Any time in her life they had gone on a trip, her dad would say, 'Make sure you pack a bathing suit.' 'Don't forget your bathing suit.' 'Did you bring your bathing suit?'

'Why didn't you go swimming too?' Alice asked.

'I came to be with you. What, don't you want me here?'

'No, I want you here, Mom. I would just like to see you have a good time. You want to get a pedicure? Bethany gets them from time to time.'

'No way! No one's touching my feet.' She shivered as if a snake were crawling down her back.

The popcorn maker looked down at Alice from the shelf after her mother had gone.

'Fuck,' she said. She took the popcorn maker and went down the hall and threw it in the garbage bin. And with it she tried to toss out her feelings.

'So, when do I get to meet your parents?' Nellcott said. Did he know that her parents had just been up? He was always freaking her out.

Nellcott and Alice were sitting on the Arts steps at midnight. Nellcott had brought his guitar without a case, carrying it by the neck with one fist. It had started to drizzle.

'The wood will warp,' Alice blurted out on their walk over.

'It'll be fine,' he said.

It was like how he stretched her shirts all out of shape when they made out. She liked her shirts unstretched.

When he mentioned her parents, she looked like she'd been slapped. 'They'd be so uptight just talking to you,' she said, her hands suddenly over her eyes.

'Come on, I don't have to stay at their house. We can rent a hotel room.'

'In Toronto? Yeah, like my parents would be up for me renting a hotel room in my own city.'

'Yeah, a hotel room.' He told her all about the hotel room they would have. If Nellcott ruled the world, there would be record players in all hotel rooms.

'And a library,' Alice added. 'For me.'

The Arts steps were located at the centre of campus and looked out at a monument of James McGill.

'You know James McGill is buried under that monument?' Nellcott said.

'That's not true, is it? That would be gross. Students walk by that every day.'

Nellcott started to play guitar. He had that ability to move his left-hand fingers all over the fret board and still look directly at her.

If he had played piano, or clarinet, or drums, or ukulele, she wouldn't have cared but she loved guitar music.

She hoped if she were ever in a coma that she didn't seem to be waking up from, her parents would hire some teenage boy with a guitar to play 'Dear Prudence' by her ear. She would miraculously recover.

Gregory played guitar too, as did pretty much every guy that came over to Nellcott and Gregory's place. Alice quickly learned what a *jam* was: a free-for-all song with no lyrics that went on forever and made Alice stare at the walls and want to chip off the paint.

They did not play covers. It was not like the park parties she heard about in Toronto where only one guy knew guitar and he played every Neil Young song he knew.

In Nellcott's living room, it was not a rehearsal. There was no one getting uptight about hitting the right notes or stopping exactly after a nod of the head.

'How'd you start playing guitar?' Alice asked Gregory while she was listening to him play and Nellcott was out of the room.

'When I heard the first three chords of the song "Gloria" in *The Outsiders* it ruined my life. I knew I was going to be a guitar player for life.'

Alice nodded. She understood.

Alice later worked up the courage to ask Nellcott the same thing.

'I don't know. My dad gave me lessons after school. I guess that's how I started.'

Nellcott and his friends had a way of fooling around by playing made-up parts and laughing about it. Alice waited to hear him sing.

'Aren't you into words?' Alice asked Nellcott one time after the jam was over, while she checked his closet for a suitcase full of poetry.

He walked past her and looked around for his lighter, ignoring the question.

'Why aren't you guys a band?' she asked him.

'Gregory and I have tried off and on but we never found the perfect singer.'

'I can't sing,' she said.

'No girls in the band. That's my only rule.'

Alice stared at him, her eyes turning into a heavy squint. That night she should have gone back to the dorm. But she found herself lying on Nellcott's bed, begging him to play guitar for her. She loved his strumming when he slowed it down a little. Then it was like a cat was kneading its soft paws on her head.

He kept staring down, not responding.

'Come on,' she said, getting up and pulling out of her knapsack a hand-held tape recorder that her dad had given her to record lectures. 'We can get this on tape for posterity.'

'I don't think so,' he said.

'Come on.' She pulled at his elbow, feeling like she was begging her parents for a Happy Meal. 'I can have it to listen to before I fall asleep at night. Do it for me. I really really want this.'

'Okay, put it in the closet so I can pretend it's not there and get out of the room.'

Alice followed his instructions and stood outside the door-way straining to listen.

He tuned the guitar forever.

Finally, he started to sing the first few lines of the Rolling Stones' 'No Expectations.' It came out gravelly and cracked but she liked it that way.

Alice stuck her knuckles in her mouth to keep from cheering him on.

'This isn't working,' he said and went to the closet. He ripped the tape from its cassette until it was dental floss.

Alice took her tape recorder back and buried it deep inside her knapsack, but it was in there and she knew it.

The next morning that Alice was in her own bed, there was no sound at all. Montreal had received its first blanket of snow. Cricket broke the silence, whooping and hollering about it at five in the morning. She ran outside to play in it.

Alice crept into Allegra's room to watch it fall past her window. She lay back on one of the purple pillows.

Allegra said, 'Alice, what colour would you say I was?'

'Raspberry bruise.' It was the name of the lipstick Allegra used. They had laughed about it once.

'Very funny. And what colour do you think Jim is?'

'Who?'

'That guy I'm seeing. The owner of that club on St. Denis.' Allegra couldn't remember the club's French name.

'Right, Jim is the colour black.'

Allegra's left hand was dangling out from under the covers. Alice noticed a gold ring on the third finger.

Alice sat up to look at it. 'Did Jim propose?'

'No,' she said. 'I wear this ring sometimes. I like to think that one day I will be married.'

'Oh,' Alice said with a pensive-eyebrows look. She didn't know anyone who wanted to get married until after they finished their degree, or ever for that matter.

A snowball hit the window. 'Wake up, you losers!' Cricket screamed from below.

'There's no way I'm going out there without coffee,' Allegra said. At this point, Alice had even seen Allegra take her coffee mug to the showers.

It was time to pull the parka out of the duffel bag. With the hood up, she had no peripheral vision and looked like ET.

'What is that?' Allegra said.

'It's a parka my dad gave me. Do you like it?' She felt like she was living inside a stuffed animal.

'It's not Alaska,' Allegra said, still wearing her black leather jacket for the outdoors.

'You could punch me and I wouldn't even feel it,' Alice said with glee. She was skinny. She needed the extra warmth.

After classes, Allegra came with Alice to a Film Society screening of *Rosemary's Baby*. That night Casey was selling tickets with Alice.

'Come with me to the bathroom,' Allegra said to Alice.

'I can't. I'm supposed to be selling tickets here.'

'Casey, can Alice come to the bathroom with me?'

'Yeah,' he said.

Allegra yanked Alice to the women's bathroom. Their trips to the bathroom together were becoming familiar. Allegra spent ten minutes putting on her deep raspberry-bruise lipstick and then kissed Alice on the cheek, making Alice feel like a substitute tissue.

Allegra left the stall door open and talked to Alice from the toilet seat. 'I know all about you.' She waved a finger.

'What?' Alice had been wondering if anyone did.

'You never sit on the toilet seat. And I go after you do and I get all your spray. What do you think you're going to get? Sit on the toilet seat, why don't you?'

'No way,' Alice said. 'Didn't you get crabs that way?' Her whole body shivered.

'Casey looks like a Roman god,' Allegra said in front of the faucets.

'Really?'

'What should I do?'

'You've never needed my help with guys before.'

'Okay, let's go.'

Allegra sat next to Casey during the movie. Alice sat in the back row to give them some privacy. She thought about how she and Nellcott had been caught making out in public lately. A few different people had told them to get a room. One woman outside the Jean Coutu drugstore had said, 'Does somebody have a pail of water?' In the dark, she hoped there would always be a place for her in the woozy part of his stomach.

In the morning, Allegra clawed at Alice's shoulder like a cat.

'What is it?' Alice said, the night still in her eyes.

'He's still in my room. How do I get rid of him?'

'You slept with Casey on the first date?'

'Is that bad?'

'It wasn't even a date.'

'Alice, this is a big step for me. I usually kick the guy out by the morning.'

'I don't know. Go for a walk on the mountain. Show him the tombstones.'

'Right,' she said. Alice went back to dreaming about birds flying by her window. Now the birds were articles of clothing.

'Why are you throwing my clothes out the window?' she could hear Casey saying.

The next time Alice saw Casey, she was with *toute la gang* at a Chinese buffet in Chinatown.

Montreal had a small but colourful Chinatown. If Alice ever had to make a distressing phone call to her parents, there was a pay phone on the corner that was battered and full of graffiti which she figured would be perfect for the job.

Once Cricket ordered some vegetarian Chinese at the dorm and it came in regular takeout containers, plastic and aluminum. Were the white cardboard boxes with the wire handles only a thing of the movies? Ever since she'd seen *Manhattan*, Alice had wanted to eat Chinese food out of cardboard boxes in bed.

She'd asked Nellcott if he'd eat Chinese with her. He said no. Didn't she remember he hated mushrooms? He hated anything that looked like slugs and Chinese food all looked like slugs, he said.

When she had gone to a restaurant in Chinatown in Toronto with her dad, the tables were covered in sheets of white plastic many layers thick. When you were done, the waiters would just take the top layer and bag all traces of your food like a magic trick and take it to the kitchen.

Alice had convinced the Film Society to go to Chinatown after one of their meetings and here they were like another magic trick happening right before her eyes.

Casey went for the dessert first. He came back with six different kinds on his plate. He jiggled his green Jell-O and made slurping noises while eating it.

'Do you play guitar?' Alice asked him.

'I play piano,' he said. 'Why?'

'No reason.'

'With girls there is always a reason.'

Alice couldn't ask about Allegra but she looked at Casey for signs of changes to see if he had been struck by a hurricane or something.

He gave her a big grin. 'Your friend is crazy,' he said. 'She threw my clothes out the window.'

'That probably means she likes you,' Alice said.

He finished his six desserts. 'Now I'm ready for dinner,' Casey said and jumped up.

Alice even used chopsticks on her rice. She couldn't play an instrument but she could eat with chopsticks. The other fork-eaters looked at her suspiciously but they did not compliment her or anything. That's something they might do in Ottawa, where you heard people were polite, but not in Montreal, where they were cool.

Alice looked at William sucking the life out of a chicken wing and Rally starting off with soup and Casey making sandcastles out of his rice and Robert with his plate that he had sectioned off like a TV dinner. She loved these people and was for the moment really happy.

William pounded his fortune cookie on the table with his fist to get his fortune.

'I don't think it's a good omen to smash your fortune to smithereens,' Alice said.

Rally read the fortune below the crumbs out loud. 'The Film Society will break even.'

'Give me that,' William said.

'The Film Society will live happily ever after,' Alice said, raising her beer. These people were her family. Even Robert, who went to the buffet table only once.

'How can someone go to an all-you-can-eat buffet table only once?' Alice asked Casey, still disturbed days later by Robert's solitary trip to the Chinese buffet.

'Don't ask me. I must have gone five times.'

Casey and Alice were showing *The Exorcist* for the Film Society's Friday-night show. Both of them wanted to stick around for the movie.

The ticket numbers were in the thirties that night.

'Do you think if we charged two dollars instead of one we could stay in business?' she asked him.

Casey jingled the cash box full of change. 'The Film Society: the laundry machine for the soul.'

The lights dimmed. 'Sometimes I just like to be in a dark room, ya know? It's like going back into the womb,' Casey whispered to her.

Alice said, 'Sometimes I watch a movie just to see how the women dress. Like Lindsay Wagner in *The Paper Chase*. It was one turtleneck after another.'

'Where's your boyfriend?'

'He doesn't like being in places where you can't smoke. How's it going with Allegra?'

'Do you know how steep that hill is to the dorm?' Casey lived off-campus. 'It's so steep, when you walk up it, your face is three inches from the ground.'

'I know. I do that hill every day.'

'I feel like I'm climbing mountains when I go visit her.'

The last time Casey and Allegra hung out together, he was talking a mile a minute, ranting and raving like a lunatic, Allegra had told her, and all of a sudden he was silent. She looked down, and he had wiped out on a patch of ice and was lying beside her. She laughed about it all night.

'Alice,' she said, 'Casey goes downtown and walks around hotels during the day, just to see what he can steal. This ashtray's from the Delta. This phone is from the Sheraton.'

Allegra seemed really happy and Alice was glad.

The first reel of *The Exorcist* went pretty smoothly. Ellen Burstyn was the concerned parent. Her daughter looked like a doll.

Then it came to the scene where the daughter threw up pea soup. Her head slowly turned and the film burned up. There were some chuckles from the crowd.

'Way to go,' somebody said.

'What?' Casey said, jumping up on his seat. He tried to look in the projection room.

After a few minutes, green vomit started to fly and then the film burned up again. Alice crouched lower and lower in her seat.

'Boo,' the audience hollered.

'What kind of operation are we running here?' Casey asked Alice. 'They're going to want their dollars back.'

Casey started running, jingling the cash box past everyone. He went flying out the door.

Finally, the film started up again but the famous head-spinning vomit scene was over.

Nellcott was there when the film ended.

'Who are these guys you work with at the Film Society?' Nellcott asked.

'No one,' Alice said. He was scaring her again.

'Well, I went by there the other day looking for you and there was this guy in an army shirt rollerblading around the office.'

'That's Casey.'

'He seemed like an asshole.'

'He's okay.'

'I bet he wants to sleep with you.'

'He flirts with all the girls but not me.'

'You are so naive.'

'He's been seeing Allegra.'

'What about the other two guys?'

'William and Robert? William is a dictator who hates me and Robert is so straight. You know I don't go for guys that clean-cut.'

'Do you guys really think you're going to be the next Hitchcocks or something? You're not even making films or anything. You just sit around and talk about them like you're onto something new.'

'What's your problem, Nellcott?'

'Don't you know what a *poseur* is?'

'Listen, if you don't want to come to the movies, don't come. I like them. It's my job.'

'It's not your job. You're not getting paid.'

Alice felt her face getting hotter.

He said, 'It's just *scenes* I hate. You're just part of an artsy scene. It's like becoming those popular people you hated in high school. Those people don't care about you.'

'They're just people. People who get old movies.'

'If you say so.'

'What if I were like you? What if I were in a band?'

'That's different. That's doing something.'

'What's wrong with you?'

'Why don't you ever call me?' he asked her.

'You usually call me. You don't even have an answering machine if I did call you.'

'You could call me at work.'

'But you're working.'

'French girls are much more aggressive.'

'What does that mean?'

'It means, I guess we're going to have to practice this. I'm going to go home now and you're going to go back to your dorm and you are going to call me.'

'Will you answer?'

'We'll have to see.' He went home.

Alice did wish she could be in a band with Nellcott. She had never been able to sing much before but her favourite band was Royal Trux which had a female and male singer. She saw them live once at Cafe Campus and usually they sang songs separately but for one song they did a duet and Alice felt like they were the rock-and-roll Sonny and Cher.

Alice checked out the signboards in the Arts Building hallway between classes. The Yellow Door was having an open-mike poetry night. The Alley was having a jazz ensemble. Someone was selling a computer.

There was a paper advertisement about vocal lessons. The bottom was frayed with the phone number repeated on slips cut like the fringe on an Indian jacket. She thumbed a slip and then it was in her pocket.

The voice instructor taught in a converted office building full of studios. Number 17 was soundproof with a piano stuffed in one corner and a mirror on one wall. She had been once to the practice space Nellcott rented in a warehouse and that had mirrors too but the floor and the other walls had huge tapestries. She missed the tapestries.

The instructor's name was Kitty. She was about forty with red lipstick and a space between her front teeth like Madonna. Her hair was over the top in a pom-pom and her voice was Minnie Mouse.

She banged on the piano with dramatic pauses. She had told Alice to bring sheet music.

Alice brought 'Heroin' by the Velvet Underground. There was a black metal music stand to put the sheet music on, which meant she would be standing. Nellcott and Gregory were always sitting behind their guitars on some milk crate or couch or something. They often closed their eyes before starting, like thinking of a wish before blowing out a candle.

'Velvet Underground, hmm. Never heard of them,' Kitty said.

Alice stood in front of the words. Kitty had gone and photocopied the sheet music in another room and was now back working it out on the piano, adding a lot of filler. 'Heroin' was not a piano song.

Alice sang it once all the way through. She started jumping up slightly when she got past the first few words.

'Interesting lyrics,' Kitty said. 'Definitely be on a note when you hit a note. Don't just wander around.'

Kitty was looking at Alice in the mirror and talking to her that way.

Alice asked, 'Do you have to look at me? I'm a little self-conscious.'

'Posture. Stand up straight like a ballerina. It'll be easier to hit those high notes. Let me hear you do a scale. Try this: e, ee, eee, ee.'

Alice started laughing and the *ee*'s were blowing out of her nose.

'Now hiss at me,' Kitty said.

Alice gave her a half-assed hiss.

'Stand up straight. Put your chin back in.' Was Alice's mother paying this woman?

Kitty sang the song once through with her piano accompaniment and everything that came out of her mouth sounded like opera.

'I've got to tell you my boundaries here,' Alice said. 'I do not want to sound opera.'

'Honey, if I could turn people into opera singers, I'd be a millionaire. You're always going to have control over your own voice.'

Alice sang the song once more and she was sure she didn't have control of her voice.

Kitty said, 'That last note. End it like a screen door slowly closing, not a door slamming shut.'

When Alice talked to Kitty next, her voice got quieter and quieter.

'You're mumbling,' Kitty said. 'You are talking through your teeth.'

'I'm shy,' Alice said, as in *Leave me alone*.

'I don't care what kind of singer you want to be. You should make sure your diction is clear and the audience hears your words.'

Alice was signed up for at least two more lessons. Maybe by the end of them she would be able to hiss at Nellcott.

She thought about telling Nellcott about the singing lessons but she just kept staring at him. They were riding the bus together because his brown car had died and he had abandoned it somewhere. 'We named the car Bernice, and then we buried her,' Nellcott told Alice.

At the university everyone was the same age, and so riding the bus with Nellcott to the suburb of Laval was like being in the twilight zone.

There was an older lady with a clear rain bonnet. An old guy with black-shoe-polished slick hair and his glasses case in his breast pocket. Teenagers with shaved heads. Teenagers with babies.

Nellcott wouldn't tell her where they were going. There were seats available everywhere but he was swaying off a metal pole. She was enjoying sitting down but felt a little naked without her knapsack.

He told her about being on the metro one time with a girl eating from a basket of red juicy strawberries and all the eyes in the metro car stared at them with envy.

She didn't feel like hearing about his ex-girlfriends.

The bus was leaving the downtown she knew and loved with its beautiful places to live in, all stacked next to each other with window boxes full of flowers and long thin metal stairways leading up to different-coloured front doors.

Then the bus was driving by concrete buildings and grey sky and chain franchises that stood alone on the pavement.

Nellcott led her to a concrete apartment building. He walked two steps ahead of her instead of by her side holding hands; he was always in a hurry to get someplace.

They walked into an apartment on the fifth floor. There was a small kitchenette, a music stand in one corner with a banjo, and framed toddler pictures of Nellcott.

Alice touched one of the photos. He was dressed up in a Superman costume.

'I always wanted to fly,' Nellcott said. 'It still pisses me off that I can't.'

Alice looked at another photo. 'You're actually naked in this one. I don't think my parents have any pictures of me naked, especially not on display.' The toddler photo of her that was displayed in her parents' living room was taken at Sears with the fake-snowflake background.

'Thanks for bringing me here,' Alice said.

They were hungry. They looked around and decided to bake potatoes.

'What do we do?' they both said.

They wrapped two potatoes in aluminum foil and stuck them in the oven.

She asked him, 'How did you get your name?'

'My parents named me after a place in France they visited on their honeymoon. Nellcote. The Rolling Stones recorded *Exile on Main Street* there. They are my dad's favourite band too.'

'My dad completely missed all the music of the sixties. He only knows about John Denver. And my mom didn't even have a favourite Beatle.'

'Don't kid yourself. My dad's no hippie; he's worked his whole life.'

His father came in. He looked sort of like Nellcott but not really. Maybe a pudgier version, but not fat. Nellcott was proud that his dad still had a head full of hair.

Nellcott's dad dragged a chair from the corner and made Alice sit down. He tried to make Nellcott sit down too but Nellcott was following him around with a lit cigarette driving his father crazy.

'Use an ashtray,' his dad told him. Then Nellcott was walking around with his lit cigarette in one hand and the ashtray in the other loosely beneath.

'What have you done? You putz,' his dad said to Nellcott, sticking his nose in the oven and sniffing. 'Did you wash these potatoes?'

They hadn't.

'Oh. Come on,' he said, tossing the potatoes in the trash with his bare hands.

Nellcott's father had a way of freaking out that Alice found funny and non-threatening. He was full of jokes and made her feel at ease. He would repeatedly ask Nellcott what he was up to these days, making Nellcott more and more uneasy. Nellcott gave only one-word answers and she wondered if she should fill in the rest. Probably not.

She hoped she would see Nellcott's father again.

Alice closed her eyes and felt like making a wish when his dad put a plate of his specialty, cut-up wieners and beans, in front of her at the kitchen table. Nellcott was still standing, leaning against the wall with one leg crossed over the other, smoking and forking a piece of hot dog at the same time.

She took a bite of hot dog and loved it. The beans gave the hot dogs a syrupy flavour. They could have been camping.

When Nellcott and Alice were in his bed together, she touched a scar that went up his forearm two inches. It was bumpy and hard like dried glue. It looked like a thick worm.

'How'd you get that?' she asked him.

'One time Gregory and I picked up these two girls on St. Denis Street and we went back to their place. Gregory went for one of them and the one I was left with wasn't too pretty so we played chicken in her kitchen with a cigarette.'

He was smoking in bed, of course, as he related this story.

'What was wrong with her? I bet she wasn't ugly at all.' Alice hated when guys thought girls were ugly. She had been ugly.

'Well, she had cigarette scars on her, for one,' Nellcott said.

Alice was thinking about this story when all of a sudden he stuck his cigarette on her right arm and sizzled it for a second.

She could not believe him.

Nellcott's apartment was always cold. She guessed they couldn't spring for extra heat. She spooned him but he did not like to be touched when he was sleeping.

In the morning, she woke up before Nellcott. She got bored staring at the ceiling. She poked Nellcott in the back. He stirred but didn't wake up. When his eyes were shut, his black eyelashes looked like stitches shutting his eyes forever.

She waited for cars to go by. She was lonely. She nudged him again.

'Fucking hell. Fucking shit,' he said and pulled the sheets over his head.

She went down to the kitchen where Gregory was mixing batter with no shirt on, just jeans. He was sharing a cigarette with Shelley the same time he was cooking. They were walking around barefoot, the soles of their feet black but they didn't care.

Alice sat down at the picnic table.

Shelley kept coughing. Alice didn't know if it was from the cold or all the cigarettes she'd been smoking or because she was laughing so hard.

'Guess what I found in our boys' bathroom?' she said to Alice, *hack hack hack.*

'You sound like Cookie Monster in a blender,' Gregory said.

She produced a rubber shark the size of a sock with little rubber teeth in an open mouth leading to a large rubber body.

'Give me that,' Gregory said.

'Now we know how the boys get off when we're not around.' Shelley put her arms around Gregory's neck.

'It's not what you think, sicko,' Gregory said. 'I've had that shark since the third grade.'

Alice giggled.

Nellcott slept through the whole breakfast and Alice missed him so much she felt empty inside. She didn't know what her problem was. She felt like he had moved to a different city.

When he did finally come downstairs, he didn't want any pancakes. He stuck his hand behind the fridge door, pulled out a milk carton and then chugged the milk straight out of the carton until it was empty.

She stared at her right forearm. It hurt where Nellcott had singed her with his cigarette. It was red and the skin had broken up a little. She wondered if it would scar. She would be okay.

Shelley found a bar for Gregory and Nellcott's new band to play, though Nellcott still insisted that they were not a band. When they walked in, the place had a homey feel with earth-toned loveseats, lounge chairs, standing lamps and standing ashtrays. Nellcott cased the bar looking for a possible place to set up. 'Where the hell are we going to play?' Gregory asked him.

Nellcott was already on it, putting his amp down on a part of the floor that had a frayed-edge Persian-looking rug. The place served wine and cheese plates with grapes on silver trays from a kitchenette in the corner. It was a step up from the beer-on-draft places Alice was being introduced to in Montreal.

'You can see the dishwasher in the kitchenette over here,' Alice said. No one seemed to be paying attention.

Gregory lurked around in a white suit that Shelley had bought him that day. With his shaggy hair and thin frame, he didn't look like a gangster or a banker, just a bluesman, and a hot one at that.

Nellcott had told Alice he absolutely refused to shop for clothes with girlfriends, under no circumstances, never. It was not cute. And he told her never to buy him clothes, ever, because he had his own style. When she reached for a tie or a Hawaiian shirt at a thrift store, she felt like someone wanted to chop off her hands.

She looked at the band setting up and she had no idea what they'd be playing. Did Nellcott realize he'd left her out of all the details?

Alice trudged to the end of the bathroom line.

She felt loved when people bumped into her drunk or when drunk guys put their arms around her. But when Nellcott approached her reeking of alcohol, it scared the hell out of her because the Nellcott she liked was gone.

'Can you hold my jacket?' he said. It was leather and bulky.

The bathroom was always a moment of meditation, but now she had to make sure his jacket didn't hit the pee-stained floor.

When she got out of the bathroom, she looked around for a spot on a couch.

There was a lot of moving wires around and setting up. There was no soundman. Gregory kept mentioning something called a PA. Bruno, their drummer, screwed the top cymbal to the stand. The kick drum had what looked like his mother's quilt stuffed in it.

Alice was wearing a Who T-shirt, from the first concert she ever went to. It had been a big outdoor stadium show at the Exhibition in Toronto. An older cousin had taken her and had sat down through the whole thing. Alice had not known any Who songs at the time but about the fifth song in, she slowly and carefully got up on her chair and wiggled around. She felt like she was wearing diapers. She felt like a baby bird cracking through the egg.

Since then Alice had seen a few more big live shows: the Rolling Stones' *Steel Wheels* tour, Bob Dylan at Canada's Wonderland, Neil Young at Maple Leaf Gardens.

But those shows were nothing like seeing your friends onstage. Seeing your friends up onstage was like seeing them with silver makeup on in front of a tinsel backdrop. It was like asking your friends to stand near candlelight and paying attention to their every facial expression.

And that was only the beginning. Then they actually played too.

'We're called the Feel,' Nellcott said to Bruno instead of the audience. Nellcott raised his elbow and flicked his wrist on a down strum and then the music was everywhere.

Bruno used brushes on the drums for the first song. The first time the hi-hat clapped together, Alice nearly clapped too – it sounded so good. She smiled to herself.

They were more serious than usual. Shelley whooped and hollered at her man by the side of the stage.

Gregory played guitar and acted as their singer too, much to Nellcott's despair. Gregory bent his knees and tipped the neck of his guitar at the serious parts.

The audience sat around in groups on plush couches. People were mostly quiet and intrigued.

A couple of girls started chit-chatting and Shelley told them to shut up right in their faces like smashing beer bottles over their heads.

Alice wished she were filming the show. She drank some beer until it felt like stars were rising up her esophagus.

When the band was done, the audience clapped and scattered. Nellcott didn't come over to talk to her until the last wire was packed away in an old suitcase.

'You guys were amazing,' Alice told him.

'We were off,' he said.

They left their set list taped to the floor. When Nellcott wasn't looking, Alice ripped it off the floor and folded it up. She put it in her back pocket.

Then Alice woke up and it was her birthday. She was twenty years old. Her mother had sent her a dozen white roses. It made her feel like she should be a star in a play. It was overwhelming. It was a pain in the ass to find something to put them in.

Alice hadn't told Allegra or Cricket about her birthday so they acted the same.

But Bethany called. Even Walker called. He sang, 'You can't be twenty on Sugar Mountain,' that Neil Young song, on her answering machine. She loved Walker for that.

She was waiting for Nellcott on a round stool that swirled at a pizza place he loved that was near the university. It was a pizza place that sold cigarettes. And when they delivered, they delivered cigarettes for him too.

He walked in. Each time she saw him, it was like he was walking into her life all anew.

'I have a present for you,' she told him.

'It's your birthday,' he said.

She gave him a cigarette pack that already had its cellophane torn off. He looked at it suspiciously.

She had taken a pack of markers and written a fortune on each cigarette. *Today you will have joy. Today you will have luck. Today you will eat something from a can.*

'I can't smoke these; the markers make them toxic.'

'Oh,' she said, confused. She had seen him pick up half-smoked butts off the street and smoke them.

She thought of her parents' gift-giving traditions. For her mom's birthday, her dad always bought an outfit from Eddie Bauer which her mom could exchange if she didn't like it. He had the same technique every year. He'd enter the store looking suspicious in his parka from 1968. He'd walk around in circles and if a saleslady who was too petite or too stocky asked him if he needed help he'd say no. He'd bounce around on the balls of his feet, touching the odd item, hopelessly lost, until he found a saleslady who was Alice's mom's build. Then he'd say to her, 'I have a wife who's about your size ... ' And he'd walk away with an outfit all boxed. And then he'd go to Hallmark to pick out a card with words on it that would most likely make Alice's mom cry. And her mom would open her gifts on her queen-sized bed with everyone on the bed watching and waiting for her to cry. And her mother would always open the card before the present and read it out loud. And the tears would always come. And she would always hold up the clothes in wonder.

Nellcott had a card for Alice and a present wrapped in a small box.

Alice opened the card first. She had expected it to say he was crazy about her. That he loved the freckles across her nose. That he loved her ears even though they stuck out a little.

On the cover of the card, it said, *Happy Birthday to someone sweet, innocent and pure* ... and when she opened it up it said, *But I haven't lost hope!* and it had an illustration of an angel losing its halo.

She froze up a bit so he opened the box for her. 'And this I bought from an authentic spiritual lady,' he said, putting a leather necklace with a pink crystal around her neck. 'She told me it'll give you sexual powers.'

What did you tell her? I'm frigid and prudish? she felt like asking him. She turned pretty silent.

'It might work,' he said hopefully.

She tried to smile.

He said, 'So, do you want to go out and get tattoos now or what?'

'Honestly, you don't even know that I'm not a virgin,' Bethany said after ordering a pizza for them. Alice had come over to Bethany's apartment to get away from the noise of the dorm. She had tried earplugs but they bothered her; she didn't like sticking anything in any orifice. Bethany's place was a monastery compared to the dorm.

'What?'

'I did it on prom night.'

'Why didn't you tell me before?' Alice asked.

'I don't know. Jeff and I just did it. You knew we got a hotel room.'

'Yeah, but I just thought that was for the minibar and a place to pass out.'

'You really underestimate me, you know. Honestly.'

'I can't believe it.'

'Exactly.'

Alice had seen Bethany's childhood bedroom back in Toronto. On her bed there were a ton of stuffed animals that Bethany had to move every time she went to sleep.

Alice had had a couple of stuffed animals too. She had left them behind.

There used to be rituals when Alice slept over. Bethany would take all the animals off the bed and Alice would sleep on a sleeping bag on the floor. Alice would watch Bethany rub cream into her elbows and then they would talk about boys. Alice would check her own elbows. They would feel like she had never put cream on them. She would cup out her hand towards Bethany for some cream like she was begging for food.

Bethany's bed now was made with hospital corners, Alice was sure. The comforter was pulled tight and there were no stuffed animals on top.

'Do you even miss your stuffed animals?' Alice asked Bethany.

'What?'

'Jeff. Were you even going out with Jeff?'

'We were friends. You know how we were. And when we finished having sex, you know, I was happy it was over. Honestly, I had one less thing to worry about.'

'I think I'll feel that way too,' Alice whispered.

'I love him. I love him,' Alice was saying. Nellcott was getting really annoyed that she wasn't talking about him.

They were lying in her bed together reading. Nellcott was reading his Winston Churchill book over again. Alice had discovered Charles Bukowski on the fifth floor of the McLennan Library and she had three of his books scattered on the top of her bed and her nose deep in a fourth. Well, Walker had originally mentioned Charles Bukowski to her but he had said that no girls ever like him. Alice was immediately curious.

'Don't worry,' she said to Nellcott. 'He's old and grey and living in California.'

Nellcott smoked a cigarette in her bed and then another as Alice kept reading. This time she didn't even make sure he was using the blue glass ashtray.

'He's an armchair philosopher. He's a fighter. He's all about noticing the sun and the rain,' she said.

'I've got to get some sleep,' Nellcott said, folding a pillow under his head and facing the wall.

Ha, she laughed out loud. 'He's so good.'

'I love this guy,' Nellcott imitated. She giggled.

She thought about the way Nellcott looked when she didn't even know she was thinking about him. One of her teaching assistants had met him and told Alice that she thought he had bedroom eyes.

Nellcott acted tough but she saw that he had bitten fingernails.

He made his own money; he had his own friends. It was hard for her to find his fear.

She had asked him what he wanted to do with his life, out of curiosity, when he wasn't living on a farm or in a van. She liked how he was; she didn't think he had to have a plan. She was just curious. He told her he had always planned to get by fixing televisions. He wanted to live in a submarine.

'Would you live in a submarine with me?'

'I like it on land,' she said.

He sighed. Sometimes it felt like she always gave the wrong answer.

He said he wanted to be buried at sea. She didn't want fish eating her.

Then he said that when he was a child he made his own board games. That he had a girlfriend with a missing arm in Grade Two. Alice thought that was sweet; she put her arms around his neck. He liked when she did that.

Alice called Nellcott but Gregory answered. She couldn't get Nellcott's work schedule straight in her mind and got frustrated when he wasn't there.

'What kind of girl does Nellcott like?'

'He normally goes for blonds. I'm the one who likes brunettes.'

'Why is he going out with me?'

'We don't talk about those things.'

'Don't tell him I called.'

'I'll tell him you called wanting to jump his bones.'

Had Nellcott told Gregory about her? She had no idea.

Nellcott had never – they had never – used the word *love*. It was just not something he did, it seemed.

Allegra had said it to her before Nellcott did. She had said it when she came back to the dorm drunk one night. 'I love you, Alice. I love you. I don't know who else I love. Let's not ever fight. Give me a kiss,' she said in the girl's washroom. Alice tasted lipstick – she hated the taste of lipstick but was in awe anyway.

'What happened with Casey? Did something happen?' Alice asked.

'I don't wanna talk about him,' she mumbled. 'Hold my beer while I pee.' She plopped right down on the toilet seat without putting toilet paper down or anything. Alice cringed.

The next time Alice saw Nellcott was at Basement Records. He took her to meet the owner in the back room. It had a tinted one-way glass window looking out on the sales floor. Nellcott went up to the owner, who stood up from a swirling leather chair behind an oak desk and whispered in his ear the way mafia men do.

Alice knew from talking with Nellcott before that he and his boss often discussed the ways of the world, and how things were, and newspaper stuff. And so Nellcott had this older mentor and that made Nellcott safer to Alice; he was someone willing to listen to his elders.

'How are you today, mademoiselle?' the owner asked.

'Fine, thank you.' The room smelled like cigars.

'So, you have met my Nellcott?'

'Yes,' Alice said, noticing the framed gold record of Madonna's *Like a Virgin* on the wall.

'He is the best manager we have, the best. You want something to drink: Coke, Diet Pepsi, coffee, diet coffee?'

'No, thank you.' Nellcott perched beside her as still as she'd ever seen him.

'So, you're in school. How is school?'

'I like it.' *I'm acting like a corpse*, Alice thought.

'And you are studying?'

'Liberal arts.'

'And your parents? How are they? Nellcott tells me they don't like him.'

'They haven't met him.'

'So why is this?' Alice looked over at Nellcott, wishing he'd help her out of this third degree.

'They wouldn't like anyone who wasn't just like my dad.'

'And your dad, what is he like?'

'My dad has googly eyes. He's a real softie.'

'He sounds like a military sergeant on her answering machine,' Nellcott said.

It was a nice brief escape to think about her dad. Her dad popped out his eyes with enthusiasm and gestured with his fingers and made everything, even getting gas for the car, an adventure. He was high on life. He was very wise but acted like he didn't know anything, so people came to life in front of him. And sometimes Alice came to life.

'Right,' Nellcott's boss said.

'I'm going to have to stop talking to my dad or I'll never be able to date,' Alice said.

'Oh, he must know that you will date?'

'He goes to movies with me. And I pick them out and they are usually about drug addicts. But he's a good sport. He can't stand rock music, though. He used to come into my room and turn off my music, saying, "Rock-and-roll music will rot your brain."'

'So, you like music. Good. Good for business.'

'Rock music saved my life.' She meant this. It got her through high school when she needed it to sleep and when she was learning how to drive a car.

Nellcott's boss leaned over to her with a finger pointed in her face and everything. 'Well, I'm going to tell you something now and you know I'm always right. Always. Ask Nellcott.' She hated guys who thought they were always right and here was another one. 'You can't keep your parents in the dark. You must call them every day. Family is blood. Blood is thicker than music.'

Alice didn't say anything. She could feel herself getting mad. 'Music is my blood.' She felt like pounding her fists on the desk for emphasis.

'Now go, go pick out any record, on the house. Nellcott will write down the number for me to keep track. Very good.' The owner squeezed her hand, hurting her knuckles.

'How dare he tell me what to do about my own family?,' Alice said once they were on the street. She had been too angry to pick out a record. 'I know he's good for you, Nellcott; I know he's probably taught you a lot. But when it comes to me, forget it.'

'Are you going to calm down?'

'I don't need another guy or anyone else telling me what to do. What do you tell people about me? Does he know I'm a virgin, too?'

'Um.'

'God, Nellcott. Lovers should not bring their love to the light.'

'We aren't lovers.'

Ouch. A pigeon flew into a sordid cloud and her hair was violent on her face and if she had been chewing gum, it would have gotten caught in her hair.

Nellcott took Alice to a diner. He was walking ahead of her again and she brooded. He loved having breakfast at all times of the day. There was always one more diner to try. She had come to learn that nobody does diners like Montreal.

When the waitress came around, Nellcott said, 'Can I have an ashtray?'

'Don't have an ashtray, hon. They're all in the dishwasher.'

'Can I have an ashtray?' he said again, thinking he was cute.

'Okay, hon. Hold on a second.'

She came back with a bread-and-butter dish that she had covered with aluminum foil. 'Here you go, hon. Okay now, what'll it be?'

'Three eggs, bacon, sausages, hash browns, a side of toast and a grilled cheese sandwich,' Nellcott said. He always ordered a lot because Alice liked to eat off his plate.

'And you, sweetie?'

'Coffee, please,' Alice said.

'Oh no,' he said. 'You have to order food this time. I'm hungry. You aren't getting any of my food.' Alice looked down at the menu a little dejected. 'Order dessert. Order one of those cheesecakes in the window with the gigantic red strawberries on top and the bits of nuts down the side.'

'I'll have a slice of cheesecake,' she said. The waitress scooped up their menus. The coffee came instantly.

'How come you like drug-addict movies if you won't even smoke a joint?' Nellcott asked her.

'I like eccentrics,' she said, letting the sugar waterfall into her coffee just to be dramatic. 'I'm not judgmental about drugs. I just, I know for me, I have a lot of anxiety without drugs. Drugs would push me over the edge.' Then her parents would really have an excuse to put her back in her old bedroom where she felt so far away from everything.

When the food came, Alice reached for the ketchup and poured out a big splotch next to his eggs. 'How can you not eat ketchup with eggs?' she asked him.

Nellcott was poking at his food. The hash browns had oil around them leaking all over the plate. 'How can I put this in my body?'

'I don't understand you. You love diner food.'

'Diner food is bad food done well; this is bad food done bad.'

She was enjoying her cheesecake. He started digging into it too. 'Oh no,' she said but she was just kidding.

On her way to Nellcott's through the snow, the temperature kept dropping but he insisted on walking. He probably didn't have the money for cab fare so she toughed it out. Thank God she had her dad's parka on, though it was beige and puffy and already had its share of coffee stains.

They warmed up in bank machines along the way. Her toes were stinging from the cold and Nellcott was making stupid jokes. She was going to lose a toe from frostbite or get a urinary tract infection or something horrible.

'Isn't snow beautiful?' Nellcott said.

They finally made it to Nellcott's place. Gregory was really drunk and when Nellcott was in the bathroom, Gregory ran under the kitchen table and said, 'Don't tell Nellcott where I am.'

Alice hated seeing a grown man hiding under a table. It was embarrassing.

'Boo!' he shouted to Nellcott and was on the floor laughing and farting and laughing more.

'We'll see you later,' Nellcott said and took Alice's hand and led her upstairs.

Why am I here? Alice was thinking and Nellcott could tell.

'You have no tolerance for silly, do you?'

'I have no tolerance for silly.' Alice had a way of repeating things Nellcott figured out for her.

Then he started tickling her, but it didn't feel good.

'Stop!' she said. 'My mother used to do that to me as punishment.'

He left her in the bed. She fell asleep easily, as she usually did, but in the night she felt for him beside her and he wasn't there. Finally, she got out of bed and looked around the house and couldn't find him anywhere.

Gregory was passed out on the couch and she woke him up. 'Where's Nellcott?' she asked. The lampshade beside him was crooked like a drum cymbal that was being smashed.

'Huh?'

'I can't find Nellcott,' she said. 'He's not in the house.'

Gregory moved past the empty bottles of beer on the table and looked all over the house while she sat on the couch.

'He probably went out. It's no big deal. You know him. He never says goodbye. He never tells people where he's going; he just goes.'

'Please, Gregory, can you do me a favour and just look outside?'

Gregory sighed and slowly put his boots on. When he went out the door, he found Nellcott passed out on a snowbank and helped him inside and to bed.

'What the hell were you doing?' Alice practically screamed at Nellcott. 'You could have died. Could he have died, Gregory?'

'I'm fine,' Nellcott mumbled. 'Just needed some air. It was comfortable.'

'He'll be fine,' Gregory giggled. He'd tease Nellcott about it in the morning.

She sat up in bed next to Nellcott's cold body. He hadn't even had a coat on. She felt like she had saved his life, that he would have died without her. But she was not happy about it.

When she woke up the next day the snow was still there. Nellcott walked out in a paper-thin T-shirt with his jacket on only one shoulder like a cape. He dug through his heart area for his cigarettes.

Alice told him to put on a hat. 'My dad says you lose ninety percent of your heat through your head.'

'We know you love your dad.'

'Don't say anything about my dad. My dad's a sacred cow.'

If you loved your dad, you wouldn't be with a guy like Nellcott. She had this thought and it saddened her. She grabbed one of Nellcott's cigarettes and started smoking it. He took it in stride like it was bound to happen.

'You could've died last night,' she said.

'Yeah.' He smiled.

She dropped the subject but the cigarette smoke crept through her.

'Why are you always studying?' he asked her.

'Didn't you like school?' she asked him.

'Gregory and I used to play practical jokes on each other in high school.'

'That's not surprising.'

'And I skipped.'

'Where did you go?'

'The arcade mostly. My mom gave me lunch money and the big decision of the day was whether to spend it on lunch or at the arcade.'

'Your mom didn't care?'

'She didn't know. And if she did, I didn't care – I was going to do it anyway.'

'Did you like any of your classes?'

'History. My teacher screamed, he yelled, he looked like he was going to have a heart attack, every class.'

'Who do you like in history?'

'Winston Churchill.' She knew that. 'I've read all the books he wrote and he wrote volumes. He had a great relationship with his wife, Clementine. You'd like her. She'd go off without him and have adventures all over the world and it would drive him crazy. You should read about that. He couldn't live without her.'

They warmed up in bank machines again. Nellcott did most of the talking while she rubbed her nose, which was already numb. It took all her willpower not to pull cash to get money for a cab. She was tough.

'I can't believe you're cold with that parka on,' he said.

'There's a loophole at the bottom.'

At one bank machine she wondered why she had to study so much if she wasn't going to be a doctor, but she did.

'You know, I was supposed to be a doctor,' Alice said. 'And to this day, I don't know how I got out of it. It's the best thing that ever happened to me, convincing my parents to back off. And really, Nellcott, the real reason I got away with it was because of a movie. By fluke, they took me to see *Dead Poets Society*, where one of the main characters kills himself because his parents are forcing him to be a doctor when he wants to be an actor. I'm sure my parents thought of it as a warning. I broke the news to them that I wanted to be an arts student that day and they went along with it.'

'So now that you're not applying for med school, you want to skip?' he said as the school gates came into view.

'You don't understand. It's like I have a thousand ants crawling in my blood all the time.'

And just like that she started running towards campus.

There was nothing he could do.

Cricket and her buddy Oliver returned to Cricket's dorm room after a three-hour chemistry lab. They couldn't have looked more persecuted.

Oliver was pale and had blue eyes that stared at Cricket's wall. He was propped up against the foot of her bed like a rag doll. He had short hair but with mad-scientist bits that mushroomed in the front.

Alice went in and sat beside him on the floor. She noticed his bright white running shoes and realized that she had never seen Nellcott in running shoes. Had she?

Cricket told Oliver she was going to the common room to study some more, did he want to come?

'No more,' he said, hands extended in front of him.

She patted him on the head and purposely messed up his hair.

Alice had never been in Cricket's room before. Cricket's rugby shoes were tied together and nailed to the wall. She had a world-peace poster above her desk. That made Alice laugh.

Cricket asked Alice, 'Aren't you studying?'

'I've got to do some Abnormal Psychology.'

'Isn't Intro to Psych a requirement for taking that class?'

'I thought prerequisites didn't mean anything.'

'Ha,' Cricket burst out.

'Isn't the Intro class just about rats and salivating?' Oliver said.

'Yeah,' Alice said dejectedly. 'I really wanted to learn about the human heart.'

'How are you doing in that class?' Oliver asked Alice.

'Failing.'

'Ha ha ha,' Cricket cackled. 'You're so funny, Alice.' And she popped Alice on the head too, though a little rougher than she had done to Oliver and it hurt.

Oliver and Alice talked so much they missed dinner at the cafeteria. They reached leisurely for oranges that were in a bowl on Cricket's desk until there were orange peels all over the floor like fall leaves.

Alice said, 'I don't think I'll be able to sleep. Do you mind if I stay here?'

Oliver said no and turned the lights off and they both lay down on top of Cricket's single bed with their clothes on.

To Alice, it was another sleepover. But she knew somewhere out there was Nellcott. Last time she saw him, he had held up a calendar and asked her if they could set a date. For sex. She said no, and then his nose started bleeding and she thought her answer caused it.

'Could you tell me a story?' she asked Oliver.

There was a huge shadow of an outside tree on Cricket's wall and a part of Alice was climbing in the tree.

Oliver told a story about his first school play. He had to kiss a girl but he was really shy.

'Every time we got to the kiss, I couldn't do it. The teacher would say, "Okay, Oliver, then you kiss her." I actually practiced on the red velvet curtains at the side of the stage. I would grab the curtains and I would kiss the curtains.' He reached out and grabbed a bit of Alice's hair to demonstrate. It felt nice, like he was petting her to sleep. 'Finally, at showtime, I kissed her on the lips and I felt her lips until I felt teeth. I can still feel it now.'

She fell asleep. Maybe she was narcoleptic. When she fell asleep, she fell hard.

'Pigs!' Cricket screamed at three in the morning, dumping their orange peels into a wastebasket. Oliver rolled over and Alice went to her own bed.

Alice received a B on her paper in philosophy and she went to her teaching assistant for help on how to improve it.

The teaching assistant acted like Alice was bothering him from the moment she walked in the door. He had black hair and a black goatee and a black turtleneck on and couldn't have looked more existential if he'd tried.

'I don't understand how to make it better,' she said, pointing to all the red marks.

'Well, you missed the point, didn't you? Go back and read the chapter.' The chapter had not made any sense to her.

'I didn't understand the theory.'

'I can't explain it more simply. A chair is a chair and you're saying it's a sofa.'

Alice looked down at her paper. She couldn't help it; she started to cry.

'You can't start crying in here and expect a better grade,' he said.

'I don't mean that,' she stammered. 'I guess I'll keep looking at the chapter and I'll figure it out.' She packed up her essay quickly and left.

Alice had come from a science background in high school and had no clue how to write an essay. Now that she had switched into arts, there was no freshman composition course to take; there was no writing centre. There were no tutors that she knew about. Just a TA with a closet office and a dying plant and an old leather chair and his name on the door and a stride in his step when at least one of his students was in the depths of despair.

I can't explain it more simply, she could hear in her mind. Like she was dumb.

She left the Arts Building and slowly walked to the library. All of a sudden, a piece of ice landed beside her with a big crashing sound. She looked up at the top of the Leacock Building. Long dripping icicles sparkled in the sun like dinosaur teeth. She could have been nailed in the head. There was a small sign at the bottom of the building: *Look out for falling ice*. What a weird way to die. She thought maybe she could live with a B.

When Alice walked into the Film Society office, there was a familiar brown corduroy couch against the wall. She looked at it in freaky disbelief.

'Your boyfriend donated it,' Rally finally said.

'How did he know we needed one?' Alice said.

'He drops by all the time. Anyone could have figured it out.'

'That is really amazing,' Alice said, sitting on an orange chair.

'Yeah,' Casey said. 'Those orange chairs were beginning to hurt my ass.'

'Your boyfriend looks like a rock star,' Robert said.

'I like rock-and-roll,' Alice said.

'Yeah, what's he doing with you?' Casey said.

'I don't know,' Alice said.

William was handing out old Film Society stickers with a symbol of a projector on them from the metal cabinet. 'Alice, I want you to survey people this week about movies they want to see.' He wanted her to go up to strangers on campus and ask them questions.

Alice was back to staring at the couch.

'Do you think you can handle that?' William stepped closer to her face.

She thought too of the Abnormal Psychology test she had to study for and the philosophy paper she had just gotten a B on. 'No,' she said.

William was astonished. She was really driving him insane.

'What do you even do here?' he said to her in front of everyone.

'I'm even failing Film Society,' Alice said, sitting on one of Allegra's purple throw pillows, cradling her knees. Allegra was rearranging knick-knacks in her room, so sure of where everything went.

Alice gave out a big sigh. 'Nellcott brought the Film Society a couch. I think I'm gonna sleep with him.'

'Is there a full moon out? There must be a full moon.' Allegra went over to her window to pull back the lilac scarf and checked.

'Is there one?' Alice went running over too.

There was a full moon.

'Are you sure about this? He's sort of a creep,' Allegra asked. She struck a match and lit a votive candle on her windowsill, burning her fingertips. 'I mean, really, Alice. What does he do for you anyway? Does he brush your hair? Does he rub your feet? Does he make you coffee in the morning? Does he pack you a lunch? Does he run you a hot bath?'

'No,' Alice said, returning to the purple pillow and hugging it in her lap like a stuffed animal. 'He doesn't do any of those things.'

'Well?' Allegra asked, lighting another candle and burning her fingers again.

'I don't think you'll understand.'

'Let's hear it.'

'Sometimes, when I'm alone taking a shower, he'll come in the bathroom and play guitar for me and keep me company.'

'Ughhh!' Allegra screamed like she thought Alice was just another rock-and-roll casualty.

Right on cue, Cricket walked in.

'Alice wants to have sex with that transgressor boyfriend of hers,' Allegra said. Alice turned red.

'Aghhh!' Alice screamed. 'I cannot believe you told her.'

'Make sure he gives you an orgasm,' Cricket said. 'I only go out with guys who go down on me.'

Allegra said, 'You're going to have to give him instructions. Order him around a bit.'

'Let me give you some vaginal sponges,' Cricket said and ran out.

'Did you have to tell her?' Alice said. 'Now everyone will know.'

'Just don't expect anything. It's either going to cut like a knife or you won't feel anything at all.'

Alice turned pale. 'Maybe I'm not ready.'

'Oh come on,' Allegra said. 'It's no big deal.' She sprayed Alice with vanilla perfume. It made Alice feel like a dessert.

'How badly is it going to hurt really?' Alice asked her.

'Your arm's bleeding. Did you scrape it on a nail in here?'

Alice looked down at her arm. A thin trail of blood was dripping down from where Nellcott had burned her with a cigarette. She thought that it had healed properly into a pencil-eraser-sized bubble but she must have snagged it on something and it had busted open. She didn't want to tell Allegra that Nellcott had branded her. 'It doesn't hurt,' she said, getting up to find some Kleenex.

Alice had vaginal sponges in her knapsack when she went over to Nellcott's the next time.

Even in his front room, she felt a draft. 'Is it chilly in here?' she asked him.

'Give me a pen,' he said.

She pulled one out of her knapsack. 'What are you doing?'

He started writing on the wall.

'You can't write on the wall.'

'Landlords are supposed to paint the place anyway when a new tenant moves in.'

She read, 'I will not complain about the heat.' He made her sign it.

She followed him up to his bedroom holding her breath. When she got there, she couldn't seem to let go of her knapsack. She knocked over one of his bread-and-butter ashtray plates with it. She bent down to pick it up.

He just watched her. He was really quiet. She thought he might be stoned.

'Thanks for the couch at the Film Society.' She wondered if he had any condoms.

'It was no big deal.'

'It was a deal, though. A good deal.'

'So much a big deal that you called me about it?' he mumbled.

'I'm not really a phone person, I guess.'

She was wearing combat boots now. She took them off.

'I just need to use the bathroom for a minute,' she said.

She could not get the hang of the sponge. She only got half of it in. Her fingers started to smell. Her whole body began to feel prickly. She was going to pass out.

'I'm going to play some guitar,' Nellcott said on the other side of the bathroom door. She could hear him go downstairs, his footsteps sounding further and further away.

He had no idea.

When she passed Cricket's room after school the next day, Oliver was sitting on the floor leaning against her bed looking drained of blood.

'Alice, come here.'

She dropped her knapsack, which seemed to be holding three bowling balls.

'Can you change the music?' he asked. 'I'm too tired to get up.'

'Help me out here – what do you want to hear?' she asked Oliver.

'The Beatles.'

'Where's Cricket?'

'At a rugby match.'

She plopped down beside him. 'I'm tired too,' she told him. She was wearing jeans and a loose T-shirt. She curled up in the fetal position beside him and closed her eyes. She felt like she had been shot.

Happy jangly music came out of Cricket's stereo.

'Can you move?' he said.

'You know, I've never been able to hear the bass in a song.'

'That's easy.'

It's always easy for everyone else, she thought.

He started tapping on one of her thighs with the bass line to demonstrate. She still didn't get it.

She panicked. 'This isn't working.' She left the room. She almost hit him with her knapsack on the way out by accident.

Later, the phone rang in her room. She let the machine get it. It was Nellcott. 'I'm at a party,' he said. 'You could be here.'

Her whole body was sore and she groaned.

Nellcott put Gregory on the phone. 'Alice, Nellcott is driving us all crazy. He's walking the streets screaming your name. He hasn't slept in three days. It's almost as bad as when he tried to quit smoking. Alice, please, I'm begging you, Alice. Throw the guy a bone.'

The library again. Alice squinted. She had fallen asleep on two hard chairs pushed together.

She went back to her dorm room and ate more raw cookie dough out of the wrapper with a spoon just to stay awake.

She looked at all her literary criticism books on *Alice in Wonderland* and Lewis Carroll on the desk in front of her and told herself she would read one that night from front to back. She had gotten to page ten and an hour had gone by. Her essay wasn't getting written.

She found herself trying to put her hair up in a twist with a pencil over and over again.

She called her parents in the middle of the night warning them she was going to fail every subject. Her dad said it was okay if she failed. When she hung up the phone, she wondered if they would blame this on spending too much time with Nellcott.

She heard her name being screamed. It took her a few minutes to realize it was Nellcott down below her window. He must have been locked out of the dorm. They locked the doors at midnight.

She tried to stick her head out of the window but it was the kind of window that opened from the top and the top of it was cutting into her neck. 'There's no way that you're coming up here – I have a paper due tomorrow.'

'I need to see you.'

'I can't.'

'Five minutes.'

'No.'

She watched him from the window. It seemed like the end in his face. 'Five minutes. But only because I have to eat.'

A pizza box with a fresh mushroom pizza that had arrived ten minutes earlier sat on her desk.

Alice let Nellcott in downstairs and he climbed the stairs three at a time to her floor. Alice dragged behind him.

Nellcott looked around. There were papers all over the bed that had on them the frantic scrawl of a madwoman who was trying to link some ideas together. He lifted the pizza box.

'Mushrooms?' he said. 'Gross.'

Alice shrugged.

He wanted to hear that she missed him, but Alice didn't feel anything just then except fear for her future.

'Do you eat any vegetables at all besides potatoes?' she said.

'Would it make any difference?'

'Yes.' She was super-conscious that he never wore a watch as she kept sneaking peeks at the time.

He picked a mushroom off the pizza and slowly brought it to his tongue. He was sincerely trying. His hand was shaking. She saw his teeth make one chewing motion into the mushroom and then Nellcott spat it right back onto the pizza.

It was a knightly gesture, she realized this, but even waiting for him to recover took every last ounce of strength from her.

After he had swallowed some of her toothpaste and lit a cigarette, he begged, 'Let's write a song together. You can sing.'

'Nellcott, it's not a good time.' She looked at him. She had no idea how to keep him.

He looked at her and then he was a door closing.

Alice wasn't proud of her essay on the Queen of Hearts in *Alice in Wonderland*. She had left it mostly until the night before and had been up all night, dipping into Allegra's coffee pot, eating more raw cookie dough and keeping the window open so the winter air would touch her spine and keep her conscious.

The essay had to be in by nine the next morning and now she was carrying it in her hands up the Arts steps, to the English department office where they stamped it: TUES DEC 5, 8:59 AM.

With no sleep, she felt sort of nauseous and her eyes saw spots around doorways and in her peripheral vision.

She sat on the Arts steps. There were other people who had just turned their papers in too, and they were shuffling their feet, slurring their words. Some of them were even in their pyjamas.

I am an arts student sitting on the Arts steps awake before noon and just the slightest bit alive, Alice thought.

Her arms were heavy.

In her Abnormal Psychology class, the professor had said that the people in university who suffer from chronic depression are the ones who leave their papers to the last minute. He had said, 'Depressives are perfectionists and by leaving their papers to the last minute, they have an excuse for not being perfect.'

But Alice didn't think she was depressed at all. She was just ready for bed but she couldn't get up from the Arts steps. She felt like she was watching the sun rise though the sun had been up for hours.

The Children's Lit guy came up and stood in Alice's sun.

She looked at him with her head tilted to the side like she didn't care about anything, but she still looked at him out of curiosity. He really was gorgeous with his white marble skin, his hooded navy sweatshirt and his piano hands. She thought the funky shades with the crazy cat's-eye tips that were on his head looked goofy. She thought he was in love with himself.

She looked right into his eyes and zoned out like she was stoned.

'You're in my Children's Lit class, right?' he asked.

I only sat next to you for a month, she said to herself. She nodded.

'What did you do your paper on?' he asked.

'*Alice in Wonderland.*' *Be cool, don't care*, she said to herself.

'I did my paper on *Peter Pan.*' He grinned like the Cheshire cat.

'On the boy who never grew up?'

'Nah, I did it on the parents: Mr. and Mrs. Darling.'

At the mention of *darling*, tears rolled slowly down her face. She looked away and brushed her fingers under her eyes.

'I guess I'm exhausted,' she apologized.

He did the strangest thing. He took the sunglasses that were on his head and slid them behind her ears.

'You know you're not getting these back,' she said.

'I know,' he said and walked away without looking back.

What the hell was that? she thought. *Why now?*

When all her exams were over, Alice called Nellcott and he reluctantly said that he'd meet her at the pizza place where they had celebrated her birthday. It was late but it was still open, bright as day. All the coffee stains on her parka showed up under the fluorescent lights. She took it off.

It felt like she was coming to a bank meeting to ask for more time on a loan. And in her own way, she came prepared. She had spent hours the night before making the perfect mixed tape for him. The last song she had put on was the Rolling Stones' 'That's How Strong My Love Is' and she meant it.

Nellcott came in late looking at her coldly. But, mostly, not looking at her at all.

She felt like she had to apologize for being the type of person who would panic if it had been more than a week since she wrote a letter to someone or since she looked up a word in a dictionary.

'That parka is so ugly,' he finally said.

'Yeah, I know,' she said, looking at it beside her on the chair. Forgetting all about the tape and wanting to cry.

'Give me it. Let's get rid of it right now.' He grabbed the coat and hung it on a street lamp right outside. She looked at it through the window in shock. It looked like a body hanging there. That parka had served her well; it had kept her warm.

When he came back, Nellcott said, 'Don't worry, some bum will take it who needs it more than you.'

Alice didn't respond, which just seemed to make Nellcott more restless. He said, 'My ex-girlfriend, the dancer, is back in town.'

'My Abnormal Psychology exam was killer.'

'Do you even care that my ex-girlfriend is back in town?'

'Nellcott, I'm sorry. I thought I was going to fail. It was too much pressure.'

'I just can't do this anymore.' He stood up, peeled out some crumpled bills from his jeans, threw them down at the table and left.

She felt pain inside but could not cry. After a while, she got up.

She walked by the parka hanging there, hugging herself in the cold. She wanted to take the parka back but a part of her was mad at it for not being glamorous enough.

She walked by the depanneur where Nellcott often bought cigarettes.

She walked by Bethany's apartment, where he once shaved.

She walked up the hill towards the dorm and slipped on an ice patch.

She walked through the glass doors of the dorm. She felt the heating system that made the air so dry hit her face on the way in. She wanted to feel the warmth so bad she could eat it.

She walked by Cricket, who was doing handstands in the hall. She walked by Allegra, who was holding a coffee pot.

When she was in her room and the door was shut, she lay on her bed and she sobbed. She sobbed so much she had to take off her shirt and blow her nose into it. She sobbed the kind of sobbing where her legs jerked uncontrollably and the bed shook with her. Her hair was messed and she looked out from it at her little room with love and she felt that when she finally did get up, she would walk like a marionette until the sun hit her.

On the last Film Society meeting before the holidays, they were picking out movies for the next semester.

'All I ask,' Alice said, 'is that you show *Harold and Maude* on Valentine's Day.' It was her favourite movie of all time. She loved how Maude had a yellow umbrella and everyone else had a black one.

'*The Princess Bride* would work too,' Robert said.

'Or *Annie Hall*,' Rally said.

'Or *Who's Afraid of Virginia Woolf?*' Casey said.

'There is not going to be a Film Society next semester since we have cost the school money. We've been cut,' William said, running a finger across his throat.

There was silence for a long time.

'Damn it!' William said, punching the metal cabinet and storming out.

Rally and Casey ended up raiding the bookshelf. They slowly filed out. Robert didn't need to take anything. The Pop-Tarts stayed behind in the filing cabinet because even Casey now found them too stale. Alice looked at them crammed onto the middle shelf. They looked abandoned.

The next day, Alice saw the brown corduroy couch on the curb outside the Student Union building. There was nothing she could do about it.

She hadn't seen Nellcott since he had walked out on her at the pizza place. It felt like she hadn't said goodbye.

She roamed the dorm floor and it was mostly empty. Students had already started to leave for Christmas break. Jim was there, though, in the hallway, locked out of Allegra's room. She had no idea what had happened with Casey and she probably would never know.

Alice stared at Jim, not understanding Allegra at all. His hair was wiry, his skin was yellow, his shoelaces were untied.

Jim said to her, 'One day a man must decide if he's going to let love take him hostage or if he has any choice in the matter.'

With Nellcott out of her life, everything seemed to take Alice twice as long and she forgot how to use the phone entirely. It took her twice as long to brush her teeth. It took her twice as long to pack for Toronto; she was going home for the holidays.

She packed CDs first. She couldn't listen to the Rolling Stones anymore. She hesitated and then offered them to Allegra.

'I don't listen to cock rock,' Allegra said.

Alice left the CDs in the hallway.

Alice had asked Allegra what happened with Casey and Allegra said, 'You know, the thing I like most about our friendship is that I don't have to explain myself to you.' Then she looked out the window at the huge cross.

Alice went back to her room and kept packing. She saw the pretty blue glass ashtray on her windowsill and threw it in the trash.

She kept starting to cry; it annoyed her like a leaky pen.

She did not want a guy to bring her down. She did not want to need him.

She stuffed Joni Mitchell's *Blue* in the pocket of her new ski jacket. She had told her parents that her parka was stolen and they sent her this old puffy white thing with navy racing stripes. She wouldn't talk about Nellcott with her parents but they knew by her short answers that he wasn't around anymore and left it at that.

Alice took her full laundry basket and dumped the dirty clothes into the duffel bag.

Her knapsack was all ready to go. It had been through a lot. It had different-coloured stains on it and the right strap was hanging by a thread. She picked it up and the strap snapped right off.

In Alice's childhood bedroom there was no cigarette smoke or the sound of fast taxis zooming by outside or people swearing in French. There were music boxes from when she had turned twelve and told her family she didn't want jewellery, just music boxes.

Alice's childhood bedroom was pink and green, the colours of spring. When she looked out the window, there were no steep cliffs or rocky seas or mountains with crosses, just driveways and suburban homes. And winter, six inches deep. There was no way she could light votive candles without her mom worrying that the house would burn down.

Alice woke up in her childhood bed extremely thirsty.

The phone rang. Alice felt like a diva chatting on the blower, as Allegra would say, in bed. Allegra had stayed behind in Montreal to look for the perfect apartment for her, Cricket and Alice. She called to say she had found the cutest place for them to live but she didn't like the name of the street it was on so she was still looking.

'Okay,' Alice said meekly.

Alice had gone apartment-shopping with Allegra once, before she took the train back to Toronto. Allegra didn't just want to look in newspapers; she had to see the place and get a vibe. She walked around the Plateau area with a clipboard looking for *A Louer* signs and jotting down numbers.

'What does $2\frac{1}{2}$, $3\frac{1}{2}$, $4\frac{1}{2}$ mean?' Alice asked.

'Half means it has a bathroom.' Allegra had done her research.

'Half a bathroom?' Montreal was different in many ways, magical different.

The Alice in the future would own high-heeled shoes and bras that fit. She would have plants that would not die. She would have a magazine photo of John Cassavetes with his arm around his wife, Gena Rowlands, on the wall. She would wear her glasses just as often as her contacts and even feel semi-sophisticated about it. And she would consider what street names could mean, personally, to her.

When Alice finally got out of bed, she went down the stairs, soft bouncy carpet under her feet. She had to go past the picture of the witch and Hansel and Gretel that had always given her nightmares. Her mother had always refused to take it down because it had been a gift from Alice's grandmother.

Alice stood in front of the fridge and heard a nasty growling sound. 'What is that?' she said.

'It's McGill,' her mom said from the TV room. That was the name of the boxer that her mother had gotten to replace her. 'He's in the laundry room. I've got classical music on for him. It's supposed to calm him down.'

Alice pulled the milk carton out from the fridge door and chugged it as Nellcott would have done.

'Aghh!' she started screaming.

Her mother came running in. 'What?'

'The milk is rotten.'

'I thought someone was dying in here.'

Around her parents, Alice lay like Jell-O on the couch in the den waiting for a decent rock video to come on MuchMusic, which was fine, except that she was like colourless Jell-O and good videos hardly ever came on.

Her dad came in the front door with bagels. They were Toronto bagels, which were a whole different breed of bagels compared to Montreal bagels. Toronto bagels had crispy outsides and soft insides; they were lighter and less sweet than Montreal bagels. Alice just stared at the one that was on her plate.

She watched her dad do it. He loved bread. He took a bite and one third of the bagel was gone. There were big tooth marks all around.

Her dad ate his Toronto bagel without a clue that there were hundreds of Montrealers out there who would yell at him for enjoying such a thing. He was all about peace and serenity and being comfortable in your own skin and he did it without even trying. She looked at him like he was the greatest piece of art that ever was.

'Go on,' he said with a full mouth.

Alice was anxious about seeing Walker. He had finished his student film about a man who goes postal.

When she called him, he told her she would have to drive down to see him. He lived downtown in the Annex, which was about an hour's drive from the suburbs.

She took her father's keys in her hand and tried to psych herself into driving. It was her old friend Walker at the other end.

Her father's car was a huge Oldsmobile. They called it *the boat* or *the big enchilada*. It was either that car or her mom's steel-blue minivan. If she ever bought her own car, it would be the smallest one on the market.

Alice drove like a granny through snowbanks, staying in the right lane with the rock music blaring. She prayed no one would honk at her and that she wouldn't have to make too many left-hand turns. When she got to Walker's house, she let out a big sigh. She had never been invited to his house during high school. Now they were in university and her friendships were growing deeper.

When he answered the door, he had the same fifties black-framed glasses but now his brown hair was streaked blond.

His mother mostly stayed in the kitchen and did not offer her anything to eat.

He took her to his bedroom. It was like a shrine to everything she loved. He had an old typewriter on his desk, an

Underwood, and a whole wall full of books and CDs. It was a lot tidier than she had imagined. Tidier than her room, for sure.

She sat on the bed and felt like a hooker, though she showed less skin when she dressed herself in Toronto for her parents' sake or to avoid her mom saying, 'You're wearing that?'

He said, 'I've been reading books about physics. I don't suppose you're into that?'

'No.'

'I was going to show you the film I made this semester, but my father's in the TV room watching the news.'

'Oh.'

'How's Allegra?' he asked her.

'Fine. I'm getting a place with her and Cricket.'

'Does she ask about me?'

'No.'

'She put her tongue down my throat within the first five minutes we met, you know?'

Alice was surprised and not surprised. She watched Walker move around his room looking for something.

'Hey, I'm still a virgin,' she told him while he was not looking.

'Nellcott had no luck?'

She started playing with her hands. 'We broke up.'

'Read this.' He put a large bunch of papers on her lap. It was the start of a novel. 'What do you think of that first paragraph? I worked on it all last night.' He lit a cigarette and reached for an ashtray from his bookshelf.

'Your parents know you smoke?'

'Yeah.'

'And you're allowed to smoke in your bedroom?'

'Yeah.'

She turned to read the manuscript but her heart wasn't really in it and it was pissing Walker off.

'Should I have the guy coming out of the restaurant or going in?' he asked her.

It could have been Nellcott waving the cigarette by her face. All she wanted was someone to be a kindergarten teacher for her, one who encouraged her to draw out of the lines, to make macaroni necklaces, to make paper-and-glue gifts that would look pretty all lined up in a row.

When Alice fell asleep, Walker poked her. She looked at the clock. It was two AM. Her parents would have been asleep for hours now.

She looked out the window. She was scared. The streets looked like Pop-Tart icing.

'Walker, I'm feeling narcoleptic. I don't think I can drive home. Do you think I could sleep on the couch downstairs?'

'No. My parents won't let girls sleep over. Are you crazy?'

'Maybe they'll understand. It's freezing out there. It's ice.'

'No. They wouldn't. You have to go.'

'Could you make me some coffee?'

'I'm pretty exhausted. Pick some up at a doughnut shop.'

Alice was at a loss for words as she stepped out his door into the howling winds. She drove with the windows down to keep herself awake and with both hands on the steering wheel, her chin an inch away. Then she was mad. She cursed Walker's name every time the car swerved on a patch of ice. She wondered if he would come to her funeral if she died.

She got home and the front door creaked, of course. The dog was curled up at the foot of the stairs and she waited for him to bark or attack her or something. But McGill lifted his head up and sniffed the air and then lowered his head back onto his paw. *Amazing*, Alice thought as she stepped over him. The third step creaked and then the seventh and she held her breath the whole time.

Her bedspread was like a body on top of her. She waited a few more minutes for her mom to come charging in and pointing out the time and then she relaxed a bit. She thought about Oliver but she thought about Nellcott more.

She lay her head back on the pillow imagining Nellcott walking from one depanneur to the other. Buying cigarettes and ripping off the cellophane. Stacking records at home. Playing piano on the cash machine at work. Going home on the metro. Reading the same book by Winston Churchill every night. Walking through the streets drinking from a carton of milk. Arguing with shopkeepers about politics. Dragging his laundry to the machines where you could watch it swirl in a round window. Peeling out crumpled bills from his pockets. Throwing stones at her window.

'Aghhh!' she screamed. She didn't know what to do with these thoughts.

'What's wrong?' her mom yelled out into the night.

Allegra called again the next night about another apartment she found for them. 'When you walk up to the apartment, each stair is painted a different colour,' she said. That was the kicker.

'What about the street name?' Alice asked before she got her hopes up.

The street name had a *Saint* in it so Allegra was happy.

Alice didn't plan on visiting Bethany while she was home. She and Bethany had drifted, as people always do, Alice thought. They had nothing in common.

'Bethany's on the phone.' Her mom handed her the receiver with an apple-pie smile. Alice had been on the couch all day again.

'Mom, I have a sore throat.'

'Here.'

'Hello? This is Alice,' she croaked.

Bethany said, 'What's new?'

'If I hear the word *adult* one more time I'm going to dive into the rosebushes.'

'So, how's Nellcott?'

'No.' She spoke in code around her mother.

'What does that mean? It's over?'

'Yeah.'

'Well, honestly, it's probably a good thing.'

'It feels like I've lost my shadow, Bethany. I'm walking down the street and I look down at the sidewalk and someone's taken away my shadow.'

Bethany was silent. Then she said, 'Jerk.'

'I don't think he even has a photograph of me and it really makes me crazy. It's like I think if he doesn't have a photo of me, it never happened.'

'It happened. I was there.'

'I'm glad,' Alice said.

'Call me back at school,' Bethany said and hung up.

Alice handed her mom back the phone and her mom hung it up for her.

Her mom was in her nightgown with the hem that went all the way down to the floor, the neckline that went all up the neck and the arms that went down the wrists. She had Kleenex up those wrists and was taking one out because *The Sound of Music* was on and it was already making her cry.

Her dad had to tell Alice to come on three times. He was dragging her to the drugstore to get her mom some club soda. Alice wanted to see the part where Maria and the Captain kiss in the gazebo; as soon as they kissed, she went.

Alice looked at the vastness of metal that was her dad's car. She was too nervous to drive again. She thought about the costs of accidents. Her father had always said to her, 'Watch it. A car is like a loaded weapon; it's like a gun. Whatever the speed limit is, you go ten kilometres below it. And no changing lanes. That's when accidents happen. Stay on the right-hand side of the road.'

She went to the passenger side. She turned the radio on to Q107. Her dad flipped it back to some concerto on CBC Radio. He pretended to be conducting an orchestra with two hands in the air, a big smile on his face and his eyes closed while he was driving.

In the drugstore, they ran into the mother of her high school crush. She had her reading glasses on and was scrutinizing the ingredients on a shampoo bottle. Alice's dad said hi to her.

To Alice she said, 'Blue nail polish?' She turned her nose up, up and away.

'How do you live in the world you do?' Alice asked her father back at the car. She loved talking with him over the car rooftop. 'Everyone's such a snob around here. You're going to have to start shopping downtown.'

'Hey, I spent my whole life working to keep you out of those neighbourhoods that you seem to like so much.'

'That woman was a witch. She burned me at the stake with her tone of voice.'

'Alice, not everyone wears blue nail polish,' her dad said. 'Admit it.' He looked at her with his googly eyes.

She wouldn't admit it. She got in the car. Then her dad got in the car.

She put her head between her knees. *Just don't say anything about rock music,* she thought.

'Not everyone measures everything with a rock-and-roll yardstick,' he said.

She was going to have her own Jack Nicholson freak-out but it passed. She looked out the window.

Then out of nowhere her dad said, 'You're going to have lots of lovers.'

Alice was shocked. He had meant it in an encouraging way. And even though she thought that she had always just wanted one lover, she smiled. 'That is the nicest thing anyone's ever said to me, Dad. I appreciate it.' She lay her head back on the seat rest and her dad drove steadily home, like a slow ship in the night.

Alice's dad caught her watching *Annie Hall* later that night in the TV room.

'Why don't you go to bed?' he said.

'Not tired.' She was going back to Montreal the next day. She was nervous.

'Are you hungry? I'll order you a mushroom pizza,' her dad said.

'Why don't you watch the movie with me?'

'I don't like movies. I like real life.' It was true. He'd go with her to movies sometimes but when she would look over at him, he'd be asleep with his head cocked to the side. When he'd wake up, he'd scrunch up his face and say really loudly, 'Is that New York?' 'Is that Chicago?' He was really into the locations.

'Don't you like Woody Allen?' Alice asked him.

'I can't stand watching him. He's too nervous. He needs psychiatric help.'

She looked back at the TV, mesmerized. 'What about me, Dad? I'm nervous.'

'You don't need psychiatric help. You need to study.'

She would study forever if she could.

Alice didn't run into Nellcott on the street that second semester, even though the heart of Montreal seemed like two streets only: St. Catherine and St. Laurent.

She was scared he'd call her name at her window or find her in the grocery store or wherever she was; he was extremely resourceful. But he didn't.

Her new apartment was feminine with sometimes a weird egg smell that none of them could figure out. They had all bought futons separately to sleep on, though Allegra didn't buy a frame and just put her mattress on the floor. And Cricket bought an extra one so they could have a couch. The rainbow steps were there every time Alice went in or out.

In the first week of living together, the roommates all went out. And, for one brief moment, it was just Alice and her new roommates Cricket and Allegra, all crammed into the booth at the Main, a diner on St. Laurent, hungry after drinking at the Bifteck. The fluorescent lights showed Cricket's and Allegra's red eyes and probably Alice's too. Allegra had her head on Cricket's shoulder. Cricket ordered potato pancakes with sour cream. Allegra ordered coffee. Alice did not feel like being crowed at by Cricket for eating *dead carcass* so she didn't order smoked meat though it was greasy and would be warm in her stomach and she needed red meat like she needed blood. Instead, she picked like a bird at the fries she had ordered. Maybe they would see the sunrise.

She wondered if her mom had ever had a moment like this where she was up all night and the sun came and it was the best part. She hoped so.

Garbage flew around the street. Drunk as they were, they kept smacking into lampposts. A guy with an over-the-shoulder bag was stapling a band announcement on one of the lampposts. Alice knew you could get ticketed for that by the police, but St. Laurent wouldn't be the same without all the photocopied band posters. One band was even playing at Basement Records.

Alice saw herself suddenly, barefoot in Chinatown, going to her favourite phone booth and frantically calling Nellcott. But he wouldn't be there, and if he was he would already be with somebody else.

The pressure of school kicked in, and the roommates each started having their own rituals. Allegra bought lotto tickets at the depanneur, which felt like a whole outing to Alice when Allegra let her come along. Sometimes, on a good day, Allegra won enough to buy another ticket.

'If you ever have a food craving, you have to honour it, immediately. You have to,' Allegra said to her while dumping marshmallows in her basket, then rosewater.

When Alice went to grab some toilet paper, Allegra said, 'Don't bother. I stole some from school.'

Alice would always remember her first big shopping excursion alone at the grocery store. She must have stood in front of the canola, vegetable, olive, corn, safflower and walnut oils for twenty minutes wondering which one she was supposed to buy.

She remembered Rally telling her about salads with olive oil and balsamic vinegar. She sidestepped over to the olive oils. There were all kinds: virgin, extra virgin, extra virgin light. She felt like screaming.

Allegra saved all her glass spaghetti-sauce jars and filled them up with different-shaped pasta and different-coloured beans and they looked so beautiful lined up on her pantry shelf. She kept her coffee and her cigarettes in the freezer.

Cricket made a lot of vegetable stir-fries. She used oil so much that one day she came screaming out of her bedroom that she dreamed she was pissing only oil. Her concoctions smelled good but she would offer some only to Allegra. The two of them ate on the futon couch with the funky floral pattern that Cricket had picked out. They watched TV on Alice's shoebox-sized television and Alice tried to walk by them with dignity as she went to her room.

Most of Alice's meals involved making sandwiches with cheese and tomatoes. Sometimes she added avocado. Sometimes she made nachos.

One time Alice tried to cook some chicken in Cricket's frying pan, and Cricket, the vegetarian, started screaming. She threw the pan on the floor. 'How can you cook chicken juices in this pan? I can never cook in this pan again. Do you have any idea how long it took me to season this cast-iron pan?'

She never forgave Alice but Cricket had never liked her anyway, Alice had finally decided.

Cricket had masking-taped the shelves in their fridge, giving each one of them a shelf, and Alice got the bottom shelf where stuff that leaked ended up. In the future, when they wouldn't be living together anymore, if Cricket tried to say hello to Alice on the street, Alice decided she would walk right by without saying a word and Cricket would not even know what she had done wrong.

Alice took some easier courses that semester, though nothing was as easy as Children's Literature. She bought black eyeliner but couldn't put it right up against her eye like some people do.

Sometimes Allegra would let Alice use her moon mug to have some tea in it and it would sit there on Alice's desk next to her stack of work.

Allegra was taking a poetry class. She wrote poems with three-dollar pens on expensive sketch paper. Alice found a crumpled poem in the trash in the bathroom and unfurled it. Allegra's printing on the page was as mystical as origami cranes suspended in air. She had written about sunsets and a fight with a boy from a balcony and the colour orange so well that Alice had to lean against the bathroom wall.

Allegra had some kind of secret that Alice wanted and Allegra probably knew Alice wanted it and Allegra withdrew. Their conversations became more and more crumpled themselves.

Bethany also spoke to Alice less and less.

And so when Alice ran into Rally on campus that second semester, she hugged Rally so tightly that Rally had to pry her off. Rally told Alice that she had gotten a job lined up for the summer repainting each and every dorm room white, one by one.

'I knew you would get a job,' Alice cried out.

'And did you know about the Film Society office?' Rally asked.

'I haven't been able to go back there,' Alice said. 'What happened?'

Rally told Alice that the Film Society office was now the polka club.

Oliver came up the rainbow steps with Alice. He had come to see Cricket but Allegra told them Cricket had gone home for the weekend and then went back in her room and shut the door.

Oliver followed Alice into her room and looked at her books. He looked at one book for a minute and then closed it in his hands, making a dramatic clapping sound.

Alice had a pair of jeans that had a big hole in the knee out on the bed. She started going through her dresser drawers.

'What are you doing?' Oliver asked her.

'I've got to patch up these jeans. I want it to look good with patterns and colour.'

She took out her Who T-shirt. It had some swirls on it and she took out a pair of scissors and started cutting the fabric.

'You're gonna regret that one day,' Oliver said.

She kept going. She cut out some fabric that had a brown floral pattern on it. She felt like she still had some hippie in her and she was frankly relieved.

Finally, she sat down with four possibilities of squares and the jeans on her lap and Oliver sat next to her. They tried different combinations of squares on the jeans and Oliver was patient and even gave suggestions. After about half an hour, she found a combination that she liked and looked at Oliver for confirmation.

'Yeah,' he said. 'Ship it.'

She laughed and put the jeans aside to sew later. She needed a break. That whole process of committing to fabric was exhausting. She lay back on the bed.

'You know, I never used the ice-cream tickets I used to get for dessert in the cafeteria,' she told him. 'What does that mean about me? I don't think I deserve dessert?'

'What? Where are they? I can still use them.' He jokingly put his hands down the pockets of her pants looking for them.

She kissed him. She wasn't there. She wasn't anywhere. They weren't nervous about it. They were playing in a way and nice to each other.

Then she lost her virginity. It was simple. It was changing positions around in bed. It was really quiet with no rock music to save her.

There was no blood even, like there was no sacrifice.

'Oh my god,' she said.

'Oh my god,' he repeated.

'You can't tell anyone.'

'Okay,' he said.

'You cannot tell Cricket.'

'Okay,' he repeated.

'You have to go,' she said. She finally understood why Allegra made guys leave after sex all those times. Alice felt like she had to be alone to digest what had just happened.

Oliver dressed with a smile. He kissed her forehead before he left.

She guessed she was supposed to shower. But she didn't.

She stayed under her blankets that felt like a layer of snow. The sheets were cool but soft.

He had left her bedroom door open. She saw Allegra come out of her room completely oblivious, walking by Alice's door-way with a coffee pot, looking like a ghost.

'Good night, our lady of the coffee pot,' Alice whispered. Alice let her walk by.

She looked around. Everything around her was full. The laundry basket, the glass of water, the moon.

In the dark, she frantically felt her arms for a raised bump. Was it the right arm or the left? She turned on the light and found it.

Finally, Alice could breathe again, and then she felt a terrible loss.

The author would like to thank the following people:

Editor: Alana Wilcox

Edit suggestors: Ken Sparling, Michelle Moore, Sharon Pratt

Writers Group of the Triad novel group, especially: Rudy Daugherty Clark, Ed Shubert, Dena Harris, Pam Cable, Michelle Hyatt, Tom Barker, Laine Cunningham

Readers: Vesna Mostovac, Peter Trachtenberg, Hal Niedzviecki, Derek McCormack, Jonathan Goldstein, Deb Greene, Courtney Beck, Celeste Houser, Andy Brown, Sandra Jeppesen

Thanks also: Mom and Dad and brothers

Broken Pencil, for publishing an excerpt from this novel in Issue 26.

Nicole Fram, Donna Shumate, Karen Hendrick, Courtney King, Stephanie Fischetti, Joree and Ken Railey, Donna Miller, Sarah Hada, Jill Kasner, Mary Dimas, Lydia Eugene, Jessica Bloch (web page designer: www.goldafried.com), one who knows who he is for my pretty montreal years, Paul McRae, Todd Swift, Sam Hiyate, Coach House staff, Christina Palassio, Justin Morgan

I am inspired by the Canadian writers I'm lucky to know, especially the poetry of Heather O'Neill, the prose of Jonathan Goldstein, Lydia Eugene, Sandra Jeppesen and Derek McCormack, the animation of Vesna Mostovac, the vision of Andy Brown, the *fishpiss* zine of Louis Rastelli and the guidance of Hal Niedzviecki and Ken Sparling. You guys are statues in my literary garden where I wander when I dare.

GOLDA FRIED grew up in Toronto and then went to university in Montreal, where she wrote poetry and was involved in spoken-word events like the Lollapalooza festival in 1994. Her collection of stories, *Darkness Then a Blown Kiss*, was published in 1998 and was listed as one of the ten best books of the year by *NOW* magazine. She has been teaching freshman composition for the last three years in Greensboro, North Carolina.

Typeset in Galliard and printed and bound at the
Coach House on bpNichol Lane, 2005.

Edited and designed by Alana Wilcox
Cover by Nicole Fram
Author photo by Justin Morgan

Coach House Books
401 Huron Street (rear) on bpNichol Lane
Toronto, Ontario M5S 2G5

416 979 2217
800 367 6360

www.chbooks.com
mail@chbooks.com